# Whistles of the Wendigo

## A Joint Task Force 13 Legacy Novel

## By Charli Cox

Three Ravens Publishing
Chickamauga GA USA

Whistles of the Wendigo By Charli Cox
Published by Three Ravens Publishing
threeravenspublishing@gmail.com
P O Box 851, Chickamauga, Ga 30707
https://www.threeravenspublishing.com
JTF-13 and Joint Task Force 13 Copyright © 2025 by William Joseph Roberts



Publishers Note: This is a work of fiction. Names, characters, places, and incidents are a product of the author's imagination. Locales and public names are sometimes used for atmospheric purposes. Any resemblance to actual people, living or dead, or to businesses, companies, events, institutions, or locales is completely coincidental.

Credits:

WHISTLES OF THE WENDIGO was written by Charli Cox
Cover art by J F Posthumus
Whistles of the Wendigo by: Charli Cox /Three Ravens Publishing – 1st edition, 2025

Ebook ISBN: 978-1-966507-35-2
Trade Paperback ISBN: 978-1-966507-36-9

# Table of Contents

For my boys

# Author's Note

When I was a young girl, my parents would take me to the County Fair every summer. We would also attend various festivals and carnivals whenever one occurred near our home in the Bay Area. Our favorite spot was always carnival row where Dad would throw baseballs at milk jugs, Mom would play the pinball horse races, and I would try my luck at the shooting gallery.

One year, I was so close to shooting out the star in the middle of the sepia-colored paper target. I remember Mom saying, "That's my Annie Oakley."

Ever since that day, Annie Oakley became my hero. I remember doing a biographical report in junior high on her. My teacher argued that my report would get zero credit because she was a "legend." She didn't realize Annie Oakley was a real person who lived, loved, and was an inspiration to so many young girls who came after her.

When Hillbilly asked me to write this novel, I knew right away which time period I wanted to set my story in. I've always been fascinated with post-Civil War America up to and including the Gold Rush and the Wild West.

I was devastated when he said I couldn't make Annie Oakley the main character. I brightened when he said, "She can make a cameo."

Perfect! The mental wheels started turning. While I may not have been able to write Annie saving the day during the climax of this book, true to her real-life nature, she was able to play a significant role.

I hope you enjoy this glimpse of a young Phoebe Ann Mosey shooting the eye out of a rabbit in order to feed her Ma and multiple younger siblings. This story is set in 1872, when Annie was just twelve years old.

In order for Annie to make an appearance, I set the story near Greenville, Ohio where she was born. Now, a cameo character does not a story make, so I researched the local lore and legends of Darke County, Ohio and found a treasure trove of Native American mythology and stories of creepy things that hunt livestock, people, and whistle under the cover of night.

If you find yourself alone in the woods at night, with an eerie fog surrounding you out of nowhere, beware. Watch out for the Whistles of the Wendigo.


Charli

# Prologue

The long winter had been a brutal one. His family had gone through the last of their food stores last week, and the local woods did not provide any fresh game. Hunger clouded his vision as he opened the door to their one-room shanty.

"Well?" his wife asked. Her cheekbones protruded under her greying skin and her eyes were devoid of their usual brightness. Straw-like hair fell away from her face as she stood to approach him.

From the corner, a cry pierced the early morning quiet, and his wife shambled over to the mattress where their son lay in a bundle of old rags.

Ignoring her earlier question, he queried, "Has he eaten?"

Holding the baby in one arm and pulling a shriveled teat out of her blouse with the other hand, she replied softly, "He suckles, but I have no milk."

Understanding dawned on him as his stomach let out a rumble that rivaled the thundershowers from last summer. His family was starving.

"Did you find anything?" she asked again, her voice pained with hunger.

"Nothing. The deer have left the area, any bear are hibernating far from here, and all the snares remain empty."

"What about squirrels?" she asked hopefully.

He simply shook his head and grimaced when the boy wailed in frustration.

"Shush young one. Shh…" His wife tried to calm the baby.

Turning to her husband, she said, "What are we supposed to do now?"

"I-I don't know."

Sensing her panic, the baby wailed again. His desperation echoed across the bare walls and sent shivers of fear along his father's spine.

Shaking his head, he turned back to the door. "I'll go out again. I'll keep looking."

His wife's face hardened when she said, "Come back with food, or don't come back at all."

The baby cried again, and she turned her back to tend to their son.

He glanced at his wife's backside. Where before, her ample hips stretched the seams of her dress, now bony protrusions barely poked the fabric. Her legs were simply skin and flabby muscle. There was no fat anywhere on her body.

A voice inside his head whispered, "You have plenty to eat right in front of you."

He spun around in confusion. There was no one inside the shack but him and his family.

The voice continued, "Look at them. They need food, and you have none to provide. Why should all of you suffer? Take what is yours and feast!"

He staggered backward towards the door.

His wife turned to him. "What are you waiting for," she shrieked. "Go find us something, anything, to eat!" There was a madness in her eyes, and he shuddered. In all their years together, she had never spoken to him like that. He was the man of the house, and she listened to what he said. *Who did she think she was to bark orders at him?*

The voice spoke again. "Look at her. Really look. She isn't your wife anymore."

A moment of clarity descended upon his shoulders. The voice was right. He had all he needed to sustain himself right here.

He reached for the cleaver on their small table and went to work. In the distance, he heard whistling.

# Chapter One

"Tell me again why we were selected for this mission," complained Private Aiden Flanagan.

"New Vienna has the Governor concerned. After what happened at the Dead Fall Saloon, he is worried about similar movements throughout Ohio," responded Private David Wilkerson.

"Leave it to a group of women to get a bug up their bonnets and try to outlaw whiskey." Flanagan sighed and brushed his red hair out of his eyes.

"There was more to it than that." Wilkerson looked sternly at Flanagan, his brown eyes narrowing to slits. "The proprietor was nearly hanged!"

"I know. I read the reports, but why us? Why are we the ones riding to Greenville? I feel like my saddle has rocks in it from riding so long."

"At least you can still *feel* your backside…" Wilkerson tapped his horse on the rump in emphasis.

"Quit your bellyaching," chastised Sergeant Wilson Taylor from the wagon behind them. "If you paid as much attention to your surroundings as you do your saddle sores, none of us would be stuck on this babysitting duty."

Private Wilkerson looked down at the trail underneath his horse's hooves and sighed. "Yes, Sergeant," he replied.

Last month, their Cavalry troop stumbled upon a Comanche camp and was nearly wiped out. After a prolonged exchange of fire, Lieutenant Peter Brant shot the war party chief, but it was a close thing.

The men learned a good lesson that day: instead of worrying about how soon they would return home, they should focus on the here and now, or else they may not make it home at all. Many Indian Tribes had signed treaties to sell their land to the US Government, but not everyone agreed, and some of the savages hiding out in the woods still had plenty of fight left in them.

"Let's continue towards Greenville for another few hours. Once we reach the creek, we'll make camp and give the horses a rest," ordered Lieutenant Brant.

The privates acknowledged and squeezed their horses with their calves to keep their heads pointed down the trail.

"Alright, men. Let the horses have a drink from the creek, then we'll unsaddle them." Lieutenant Brant hopped down from the buckboard and staggered to a nearby tree to relieve himself. He was in charge of this regiment until they reached Greenville. At that point, he would link back up with his Special Unit to continue their primary mission: Holding the line between Heaven and Hell. Until that time, he needed to ensure the safety of these men and their supplies.

Captain McLellan recommended Brant for this mission. It didn't hurt that the men with him were all from Ohio and knew the territory. *If I never meet another Comanche again, it will be too soon.*

Brant shuddered at the memory. *As long as the men keep their wits about them, and we don't get ambushed, we'll make it safely to Greenville in no time.*

"Sir? Those Oaks look to already have a high line," commented Private Wilkerson.

"Good eye, Private. Check the rope for fraying and if it is intact, use it for our mounts."

"Yes, Sir."

Private Wilkerson examined the rope and found it serviceable. He unsaddled his trusty Morgan gelding and gently dropped the headstall of his bridle over his ears. Dawson released the bit and stuck his tongue out. Chuckling, the private pulled gently on his tongue in their favorite game after a long ride. Dawson rubbed his forehead along Private Wilkerson's shoulder, a way to show affection for the attention of his rider.

Wilkerson ran a brush over Dawson's withers and along his back, removing as much dried sweat and caked dirt as possible. No matter how sturdy the saddle blanket, dust and grime always managed to find its way to his horse's coat. Concluding the grooming with a pass over his rump and down his hind legs, Private Wilkerson placed the brush in his leather saddle bags and retrieved the dull knife he kept at the ready.

He ran his hand down the back of Dawson's foreleg and gently squeezed just above the fetlock. The bay gelding obligingly lifted his hood off the packed ground and allowed the private to pick out any rocks and mud from around his frog. Satisfied, he turned his attention to the other foreleg and then both of his hind legs.

As soon as he gently set the last hoof back onto the ground, Dawson snorted. Darkness descended over their camp and the air grew thick and still. From the distance, someone whistled.

The crisp melody sent a shiver down Private Wilkerson's spine that caused his hackles to rise underneath the collar of his uniform.

Dawson snorted and pawed at the ground. The other horses reacted similarly, heads up, ears pricked, and eyes alert.

"Sir!" Private Flanagan called to the lieutenant. "Something is out there."

"Set a perimeter!" ordered Lieutenant Brant. Keeping the horses in the center, the men shouldered their Henry Sharp rifles and pointed them into the surrounding woods.

The only sound Private Wilkerson could hear, besides the pounding of his own heart, was a distant rustling in the underbrush.

The other men stiffened in anticipation. Their eyes darted around, but without sunlight, there was not much any of them could see.

One of the horses squealed and pulled away from the high line. The red mare's halter slipped off her head leaving her free of the restraint. She bolted into the dark, the other horses whinnying and snorting in fear. They stamped and pawed at the ground in annoyance, but none of the others panicked as she had.

Private Wilkerson approached Dawson and gently patted his shoulder. His bay coat was soaked with sweat and the muscles under his skin were drawn taut. David felt like he was patting a rock, not his mount.

As he pulled his hand away, Dawson reared up, forelegs thrashing in the air fractions of an inch above the private's head. "Whoa, now. Easy, Boy!" Private Wilkerson tried to soothe his panic before a shod hoof found purchase.

Sidling out of the line of fire, he approached their corporal. "If we can't calm the horses, we will lose more than just the mare."

"I know, Private, but they're all spooked." Corporal Ethan Miller replied. "These are well-trained war horses. They have been in more battles and road marches than I can count. If they're afraid, we should be, too."

A sharp whinny pierced the darkness followed by a growl. It sounded close, but distance was impossible to measure due to the oppressive darkness that surrounded them.

Private Wilkerson heard a thwack, then a snort, and then silence. The lack of sound was deafening. After a few heartbeats, the air thinned and he was able to see faint beams of moonlight shine throughout the woods.

The men exhaled in unison as the horses ceased panicking and nibbled at the ground.

Dawson nuzzled Wilkerson's shoulder, still breathing hard, but the whites that were prominent in his eyes moments ago were now gone.

Lieutenant Brant called out, "Everyone alright?"

The cavalrymen responded one by one, and none were missing.

"Sir, I need to retrieve my mount," said Private Flanagan. He had to crane his neck back in order to look the lieutenant in the eyes.

"Not tonight, son. Whatever had the horses so spooked might still be out there. We'll set a security schedule for the night and move out at first light. Wilkerson, you take first watch."

"Understood, Sir."

Sunlight peeked over the distant hills, warming Private Wilkerson's fingers as he stooped over the fire. Private Flanagan approached him from behind, his face ashen and eyes bloodred.

"Here," said David. He handed him a mug filled with dark encouragement.

"Coffee? Oh, thank you. I didn't sleep a wink last night."

"I could tell. Worried about your mare?"

"Yes, I need to find her. There is no way I can make the rest of the journey on foot."

"We have the wagon."

"I know, but I'm a Cavalryman. Without my mount, I'm just a soldier."

Private Wilkerson nodded in understanding. Being in the Cavalry was more than just riding on horseback. There was a symbiotic relationship between mount and man. They were a team, dependent on each other not only for completion of the mission, but for survival as well. Without a horse, they had no purpose. Sure, they could fight on their feet, but their training incorporated mounted tactics. A man on foot couldn't charge a line of Rebels as effectively as he could while astride.

Private Wilkerson took a sip of coffee and sighed in contentment. It had been a cold night, mist from the horses' breathing created a low fog over their camp. Sleep had been difficult for all the men. Even though sentries had been posted, none of the others felt truly at ease. The horses also seemed restless, switching their weight from rear hoof to rear hoof as they stood hip-shod at the highline.

In the dawn's early light, the horses seemed more rested, eyes drooping, and ears flicking around at distant chittering and chirps of the birds around them.

Private Wilkerson finished his coffee and poured more for Flanagan. "Drink this, and I'll ask if we can search for your mare."

"Thank you. I'm worried sick about her."

David placed a hand on Aiden's shoulder and gave him a gentle squeeze of understanding.

He strode purposefully to the tent where Lieutenant Brant was preparing the group to depart. Clearing his throat softly, he came to attention and waited to be acknowledged.

Lieutenant Brant looked up. "At ease. Come in, son. What can I do for you?"

"Sir, Private Flanagan's mare ran off last night and he is distraught with worry. Would you mind if I went with him to find her?"

"We should be packed up and out of here within the hour, so be quick about it. Hopefully, she didn't end up in an Indian camp."

Private Wilkerson blanched. "That hadn't occurred to me, Sir."

"Saddle up your mount and take Corporal Miller with you. Have him mounted, as well. Private Flanagan can go on foot."

"Yes, Sir." He came back to attention.

"Dismissed."

Wilkerson went back to the fire and told Flanagan to get ready.

"I was born ready." He grinned.

Corporal Miller came over to the fire. "What news?"

Wilkerson answered, "The lieutenant permitted us to look for Flanagan's mare. He said you should come with us. Here, have some coffee first."

"Much obliged. Would you mind getting Beau saddled for me?"

"Not at all. Enjoy the coffee. I'll bring the horses 'round in a jiffy."

Wilkerson quickly brushed down both Dawson and Beau and swiftly saddled them. Where Dawson's coat was brown with a black mane and tail, Beau's was black. His normally cream-colored mane and tail were brown with dust from the long ride. Under his breath, he muttered, "I'll get that dust brushed out of there when we stop in Greenville."

Beau nickered and playfully nipped at his wrist with his lips. "Alright, enough of that. We have a job to do."

Both horses appeared to sober, almost as if they understood his words. They stood patiently while Wilkerson inspected their hooves for any rocks that may have gotten in there during the restless night.

"OK, boys, we are ready."

He led the horses to the campfire where Corporal Miller and Private Flanagan were waiting. Corporal Miller patted

Beau's barrel twice as he tightened the girth. "Nice try, old man," he said with a grin.

Wilkerson chuckled as he did the same with Dawson's saddle.

They mounted up and rode out of the camp, with Private Flanagan in the lead on foot. After a few hundred paces, he stopped short. Aiden looked down at the brambles beneath his feet and underneath limbs hanging from the forest trees.

"I think I see blood." He pointed to a dark splotch on the leaves of a Bloodroot bush.

Wilkerson dismounted to check, pulling the reins over Dawson's head so he could graze.

They walked on until they found a tree limb lying on the ground. It was about a foot in diameter, the bark ragged where it had broken away from the trunk. Smaller branches were cracked along its length and the leaves were black with what appeared to be tar.

Flanagan leaned forward to get a closer look, but Wilkerson stopped him.

"That doesn't look like blood. Don't touch it!"

From behind them, Corporal Miller whistled. They spun around and found him pointing off into the distance. "There is something out there." He lowered his gaze at Flanagan and said solemnly, "Stay here. Wilkerson, you're with me."

Private Flanagan protested, but the corporal made his intent clear when he said, "That's an order."

Aiden visibly deflated, but was able to mouth the words, "Yes, Sir."

"Don't call me 'Sir!'"

Wilkerson chuckled at the exchange. A harsh glare from Corporal Miller caused his quaking sides to still immediately.

Wilkerson pulled his Remington New Army revolver from his belt as Corporal Miller led them underneath a copse of birch trees. When they reached the center, the stench of copper made both their mouths water. Bile crawled up Private Wilkerson's throat and he had to swallow repeatedly to keep himself from vomiting.

Corporal Miller took a handful of deep breaths before continuing.

Their feet crunched across dried leaves strewn about the game trail. Dead limbs reached for them as they staggered underneath, snagging their collars, and threatening to pull the caps off their heads. As they approached a clearing, everything grew eerily quiet. The earlier bird noises all but ceased, replaced by the thundering of their hearts pounding in their ears.

Pockets of mist enveloped them as they stalked towards the center of the clearing. Their clothes grew damp with the fog as it mixed with their sweat. Their trousers clung to their legs as they moved, almost tripping with the effort of placing one booted foot in front of the other.

Suddenly, Corporal Miller stopped, Wilkerson placing a hand between his shoulder blades to avoid crashing into him.

"What is it?" he asked in a harsh whisper.

"I think we found Red's mare, at least what is left of her."

"You know he hates being called that, right?"

The corporal gave a curt nod. "He can't hear me right now."

Wilkerson peered around Corporal Miller's shoulder and shuddered. A large rib cage gleamed in the morning light.

Chunks of flesh lay in mangled piles all about the space. As they drew closer to the horrific sight, the stench of blood and death grew stronger.

Wilkerson was no longer able to control his stomach. He heaved, the coffee from earlier violently ejecting from his mouth and nose as he fought for breath.

"Easy there. Calm down. Don't fight it. Let it out." The corporal tried to ease David's plight as he controlled his own breathing.

Red called out from behind them. "Did you find her?"

Wilkerson nodded after he coughed his last and Corporal Miller turned back to where they had left Red and the horses.

"We did."

"How is she? Is she scared? Let me see her." Red ran up to them, the other mounts forgotten in his excitement to check on his mare.

Corporal Miller held both arms out in front of Red. He shook his head solemnly and said, "Trust me. You don't want to see this."

Red collapsed to his knees, hot tears streaming down his face.

Wilkerson walked over to Red and put a consoling arm around his shoulder. Helping him to his feet he said, "Come on. We need to get back to the others. Whatever did this couldn't have gotten far."

The corporal nodded and led them back to the trail where Dawson and Beau grazed on some tall grass, as if nothing strange had happened in the night.

"Took you long enough!" Lieutenant Brant let his irritation with the missing men show as he watched them return to camp. He narrowed his green eyes at them as they approached. "We were about to mount up and leave you behind." One look at their forlorn expressions, and he realized what had happened. He looked at Red and asked, "Are you alright?"

Red sniffed and wiped his eyes with his shirt sleeve. "No, Sir, far from it. She was my responsibility and I failed her." He sobbed again and was unable to meet the lieutenant's soft gaze.

"No matter how much time we spend, how many hours of training, these horses are still prey animals, bound by their instincts and prone to flight. It's not your fault."

"I understand if you need to dock my pay, Sir." Red sniffed.

Lieutenant Brant gripped both of Red's shoulders and squeezed slightly, forcing Red to look up into his eyes.

"Don't worry about that right now. We are already behind schedule. Let's get a move on, or we'll never make Greenville by nightfall."

Red nodded and walked towards the wagon. There was no way he would be able to keep up with their horseback column if he was on foot. Sergeant Wilson Taylor, aka "Cookie" gave him a nod and a hand up onto the buckboard.

Cookie clucked his tongue and the team pulling the wagon started down the trail.

Red searched their surroundings looking for any sign of whatever had attacked them last night. He jumped at shadows and continuously reached for his revolver ready to draw at the first sign of a threat.

After about an hour into their journey, Cookie grabbed Red's knee. "Son, you need to stop. Your anxiety is putting fear into the wagon horses. I appreciate you being alert and all; however, making the rest of the horses nervous will do nothing to bring your mare back. Even worse, we could lose the rest of the mounts. Close your eyes and try to get some rest."

Red opened his mouth to protest, but Cookie cut him off.

"This wagon is my responsibility. I will not have you putting it and the lives of everyone else in danger. You hear me?"

Red's cheeks flushed with embarrassment. Cookie was right.

He sighed. "I hear you."

# Chapter Two

The early morning mist settled on the clearing just as the first rays of daylight appeared over the distant foothills. Phoebe checked her rifle as she lay in the prone waiting for the local varmints to make an appearance. Times were tough and it was her job to collect meat for her family. Any extra was brought to the G.A. Katzenberger & Bro. store where Mr. Katzenberger would sell it to restaurants and hotels in Cincinnati. He was kind enough to add the value of the game to their account.

Ma did her best to provide for Phoebe and her six siblings; however, every little bit helped. As she thought about her hungry brothers and sisters back at the house, she saw movement off to her right.

Phoebe scanned below the shrubs and saw a rabbit hopping tentatively out of its burrow. She waited for it to get more into the open so she could take a clear shot.

Aiming her pa's old muzzle loader, she slowly pulled the hammer to full cock and held her breath. The rabbit took another half-hop, and she squeezed the trigger.

*Boom!*

Her bullet flew true and hit the rabbit in the eye. It fell sideways and stilled. Instead of rushing forward out of her position, she waited. Sure enough, a couple more rabbits emerged to see what caused the ruckus. She reloaded the long gun, placed the percussion cap on the nipple, aimed, cocked the hammer, and waited. As the rabbits hopped next to each other, Phoebe fired and dropped both of them with one shot.

After hesitating another few minutes, she decided no more rabbits would show themselves. Phoebe crept forward, careful not to spook any other wildlife in the area, and placed the three rabbits into her game bag. She tied it closed and made her way back to her family's small cabin.

As she walked along the well-worn game trail, she noticed it was eerily quiet, even for the early hour. Usually, the whippoorwills would be up and about, chirping merrily as they hunted for bugs and worms. The robins would be pecking at the ground, pulling up worms to bring back to the babies in their nests.

Phoebe walked on but decided to pay more attention to her surroundings. It wasn't unusual for her to be out in the woods by herself, she was thirteen years old after all, but it wouldn't do her family a lick of good if she, and more importantly, her hunt, didn't make it back.

With that thought, she quickened her pace, her breath coming more heavily as she rushed back home. As she approached the cabin, the hairs on the back of her neck stood up. She stopped abruptly and hid behind the trunk of a sugar maple tree.

The local woodsman had mentioned seeing signs of wolves in the area. If they smelled the blood from the rabbits she harvested, it was possible they would follow her for a quick and easy meal. Last winter was less forgiving than usual and more than one family had disappeared during the harsh season. Phoebe tried not to think about that right now. She had to focus.

Clearing her mind, she listened to the quiet. The birds were still silent, and she couldn't hear anything more than the early morning breeze rustling the leaves around her. Steeling herself, she left the concealment of the tree and crossed the yard to her front door. As her hand pushed the door open, she heard whistling in the distance.

# Chapter Three

"Samson, how is our stock looking?" Mr. Katzenberger asked his longtime helper. Samson had worked there for many years, through the lean winters and muddy spring seasons. An order had just been delivered from Cincinnati and he trusted Samson to check everything for quality as well as quantity.

Their previous supplier had shorted him on more than one order. Samson had been diligent and caught the discrepancy before Mr. Katzenberger made payment. For that, the store owner was grateful.

This new supplier had been trustworthy so far, but trust was something easily broken. There was no harm in verifying the contents of the delivery. Speaking of…

"Aren't we waiting on a Cavalry troop?" Mr. Katzenberger hollered towards the back of the store where Samson was checking the order with the packing list.

"Yes, Sir. They should be here any minute."

Just then, his door swung open, the bell hung in the jam tinkling at the prospect of a new customer.

"Welcome to my mercantile. How can I help you?" Mr. Katzenberger offered his hand in greeting.

Lieutenant Brant took his hand and gave it a firm shake.

"Thank you, Sir. My troop is here on a mission. I trust the telegraph office sent you a list of our needs."

Mr. Katzenberger chuckled. "I should be calling you 'Sir' Lieutenant. Yes, I have your order in the back. Please, follow me." He ushered the lieutenant to the back of the store where he introduced Samson.

Samson bowed at the lieutenant but did not accept his offered hand. Instead, he reached down to the order list and started marking off items as he went.

"Yes, that sounds correct. Much obliged." The lieutenant again reached for his hand, but Samson handed him the list for a signature.

The lieutenant turned to Mr. Katzenberger. "Everything appears in order. On behalf of the US Army 6th Regiment of Cavalry, we thank you for your assistance."

Mr. Katzenberger smiled and grasped the lieutenant's hand. "Happy to help our boys who are working to keep us safe." His eyes glittered. "Pull your wagon around back and Samson will get you loaded."

Lieutenant Brant looked at Samson then shook his head. "That won't be necessary. My men can handle it. I wouldn't want to take up any more of Samson's time."

"Very well." Mr. Katzenberger smiled. He led the lieutenant through the back door and outside to the waiting wagon.

The lieutenant instructed his men to load up the supplies. Cookie and Red jumped off the buckboard and started placing boxes into the back.

"Mr. Katzenberger? If I may impose upon you for a moment further?"

"Of course. What do you need?"

"On our journey here, we encountered something strange. Could you direct me to the telegraph office?"

"Of course, Sir. There have been rumors of strange happenings in the local woods. Perhaps, I can shed a light."

Lieutenant Brant considered for a moment. "Perhaps, but I'd like to report the incident first. When I return, I would appreciate any information you can give me."

"Of course." Mr. Katzenberger pointed up the road to the telegraph office.

The lieutenant pulled Corporal Miller aside. "Come with me."

"Yes, Sir." The Corporal handed the box he was holding to Red and followed the Lieutenant down the street.

After they were out of earshot of the rest of their men, Corporal Miller asked, "What do you need from me?"

"You saw what was left of Red's horse after whatever it was attacked us. I need you to help me describe it when I make my report."

"I'm happy to help, Sir, but I didn't see anything. All that was left was a ribcage and a pool of blood."

"I understand, but the more information you can give me, the more seriously our report will be taken."

"Understood, Sir."

They walked purposefully along the boardwalk and crossed the threshold into the telegraph office. As the door creaked closed behind them, Lieutenant Brant came up short.

"Cash, is that you?"

Corporal Cash chuckled and walked over to the Lieutenant. "Sir, it's good to see you."

"And you. What are you doing here?"

"Just passing through. How about yourself?"

"It seems the womenfolk in New Vienna didn't take kindly to their men spending so much time in the saloon. They started a 'Temperance Movement,' and the Governor is concerned it may make its way here to Greenville. My regiment is tasked to keep an eye on things to prevent any of the local women from causing any problems here."

Lieutenant Brant introduced Corporal Miller to Cash.

He leaned into Cash's ear and said, "We encountered something strange on the way here."

Cash raised his eyebrows and whispered, "Strange how?"

"An odd mist descended upon our camp along with an eerie silence. The horses spooked and one of them ran off into the woods. Miller here went with a couple of our privates to find her the next morning, and only found her remains."

Cash pondered for a moment, then asked, "Could it have been a bear?"

Corporal Miller said, "No. Bears give off a distinctive odor. They smell musky, like a wet dog. Whatever this beast was, there was no scent I could discern. All I could smell was the stench of death and decay."

"I see…," said Cash. "Let me speak with my unit once my leave here is concluded. We may be able to shed some light on the situation."

"I would appreciate that," said Lieutenant Brant as he grasped Cash's hand.

The Lieutenant made his way to the operator and sent his message:

*En route to Greenville, we were attacked by an unknown creature. Private Flanagan's mare ran off and her remains were found the next morning. The creature stripped her bones clean and only left frayed bits of skin. All organs and meat were gone, presumably ingested.*

*We will remain in Greenville on our primary mission unless ordered otherwise.*

*Lieutenant Peter Brant*

He finished his report with a sigh. "Corporal, anything to add?"

Miller reviewed the report and shook his head. "No, Sir. Looks like you covered it."

Lieutenant Brant thanked the operator, and they made their way back to the General Store.

Lieutenant Brant verified the wagon was loaded and rallied his men before they set off. As they gathered around him, he opened his mouth to speak but was distracted by a teenage girl sprinting through the street.

Her boots skidded along the dirt as she slowed in front of the mercantile. Bending over to catch her breath, chest heaving and eyes wide, she noticed the Cavalry and flushed.

The lieutenant called out, "Are you in danger? Do you require assistance?"

She shook her head. "No, thank you, Sir. I just need to speak to Mr. Katzenberger." With that, she took another deep breath and walked purposefully to the door.

Lieutenant Brant noticed the sack she had slung across her back. Dark red splotches gathered at the bottom, evidence of a successful hunt. *That is interesting…* he thought.

The lieutenant heard the ting of the bell as she entered. He motioned to Corporal Miller and Private Wilkerson. "Come with me. This young girl might know something about our strange beast."

When they entered the store, they found the girl pacing in front of the counter. She started when the men entered.

"Are you sure you are alright?" asked the lieutenant again.

"Yes, Sir. I'm certain. I just need to speak with Mr. Katzenberger."

"Mr. Katzenberger is indisposed at the moment. May I help you?" asked Samson.

The young girl opened her mouth, then shook her head, as she seemed to think better of it. "No, Mister. Ma said I am only to deal with Mr. Katzenberger."

"You are welcome to wait, but he won't be available for a while."

"How long is a while?"

"Hard to say. Are you sure I can't help you?"

Sensing the girl's discomfort, Lieutenant Brant approached the counter. "Samson, was it?"

The young man behind the counter nodded. For the first time, the Lieutenant noticed his pale skin and glassy eyes. Sweat beaded on his forehead and he wiped it absentmindedly with his pale-yellow shirtsleeve.

"That's right." He answered with gravel in his voice. Earlier, Samson seemed quite efficient, if reluctant to take the Lieutenant's offered hand. Now, he seemed a completely different man altogether.

"Perhaps, I can help the young Miss…"

"Phoebe, Sir. Phoebe Ann Mosey, but everyone calls me Annie."

Upon closer inspection, the young girl looked about thirteen years of age. Dust and dirt covered her clothing and dried blood coated her hands. He understood immediately.

Back in his hometown, youngsters would hunt wild game and bring their hunt into town for trade. Each varmint had its own value depending on size, weight, and the amount of meat. Some were valued for their pelts, especially rabbits.

Times were tough during and after the Civil War, so everyone had to pitch in to make ends meet. Having children hunt was a way for them to assist their parents in providing necessities for their families, especially during a long hard winter.

The lieutenant gave Annie a warm smile. "Miss Annie, have you come here to trade?"

She stammered. "Y-yes, Sir, but my Ma said to only deal with Mr. Katzenberger. They have an arrangement."

"I see, and Mr. Samson here cannot assist you?"

"No, Sir, Ma was adamant. She and Mr. Katzenberger have an understanding."

The lieutenant looked at Samson. "I just spoke with him a few minutes ago. He was going to help me with something when I returned. Are you certain he is unavailable?"

"Quite." Samson clipped the 't' in his response.

"Very well, then. Does Mr. Katzenberger keep records of these understandings?"

Samson blanched further and shook his head. "No, he seems to know what value every trade is worth at the given moment. He has not shared his methods with me."

Lieutenant Brant looked back to Annie. "Samson said Mr. Katzenberger won't be back for a while. How long are you prepared to wait?"

She shifted on her feet and fidgeted with the strap of the burlap sack across her back.

Lieutenant Brant continued, "Surely your Ma would approve of you dealing with a Cavalryman in Mr. Katzenberger's absence?"

Annie brought her index finger to her chin in contemplation. After a moment's hesitation, she nodded.

"Very well, why don't we go out front and you can show me what you have there."

"Yes, Sir. Oh and Mr. Samson, would you please let Mr. Katzenberger know I stopped by?"

Samson nodded and returned to the back.

Once they were outside, the lieutenant led Annie to the waiting wagon.

"What do you have there?"

Annie slung the bag from over her shoulder and worked the knot tying it closed. She opened the mouth of the bag wide and reached inside. Fiddling around a bit, her hand emerged wrapped around two rabbit ears. The large hare measured about three feet in length from forepaw to hind, and despite the harsh winter, had plenty of meat on its bones.

Private Wilkerson whistled in approval. "Did you hunt that yourself?"

Annie huffed. "Yes, I did. Took it with my Pa's old muzzleloader. There are two more in here from yesterday."

She pulled out the other two and they also were large with plenty of meat.

Cookie came over and asked, "Sir, can we bring her along with us? With all that fresh game, I can make us some good grub." He patted his rotund belly.

Red added, "No offense to Cookie's skills, but field rations all start to taste the same after a while."

Lieutenant Brant shook his head. "No fellas, we can't take her with us. Her ma will get to wondering where she went. Perhaps, we can give her a ride home, though?" He looked at Annie to gauge her reaction.

"That might be best. That way you and Ma can haggle over the rabbit meat and skins. She knows their value better than me."

Lieutenant Brant nodded, and Corporal Miller gave her a boost onto the buckboard between Cookie and Red. "Alright, men. Move out!"

As it turns out, Annie's home was not far from where the men made camp last night. A game trail Annie knew well proved a shortcut from her shack into town. The wagon couldn't follow it, so she showed them the long way around, over the creek, through a couple of wooded groves, and finally to a small, cleared lot where a dilapidated shanty stood, barely.

Lieutenant Brant's horse led the wagon down the narrow shadowed drive.

At the approach of the wagon, a woman threw the door open and leveled a breechloading shotgun. She screamed, "State your business!"

The men all reached for their revolvers, but Annie stood up with her hands raised high.

"Ma! It's me. These men brought me home to trade."

"Trade?" she asked without lowering her scattergun.

"Yes, Ma. Mr. Katzenberger was out, and you told me to only deal with him. Samson didn't know when he would be back, so the lieutenant here offered to bring me home so as I could trade with them instead. Only I don't know what you want for the rabbits, so I figure you can speak with them."

The woman's eyes shrank ever so slightly, and she lowered her weapon. All the men visibly relaxed.

"Very well then. Annie leave your sack and go inside. You look a mess."

"Yes, Ma. She hopped down with Corporal Miller's help and started running towards the shack. Before she reached the door, she called over her shoulder, "Thank you for the ride home, Sir."

Lieutenant Brant tipped his hat, which caused Annie to curtsey before turning back around and going inside. From beyond the threshold, more children's voices were heard, although the men couldn't make out the words.

The lieutenant stepped forward and extended his hand. Annie's ma hesitated, but took his hand gently, keeping a wary eye on the other men in the wagon and on horseback.

"You said you came here to trade?" she asked skeptically.

"Yes, Ma'am. Your Annie is quite the hunter. Those rabbits are quite a find."

"That's my girl. If it wasn't for her, I don't know how I would keep everyone fed."

"You have many more children?"

She nodded. "Six of them."

"That is quite the houseful. Do all of them hunt?"

"And just how is that any of your business," she looked at his rank insignia, "Sir?"

Lieutenant Brant placed his hands in front of him in a placating gesture. "No offense intended, Ma'am."

"Humph," she retorted. "Now, about that trade."

"What do you think is fair for those rabbits?"

"They are rather large and have a good amount of meat on them, so I think a dollar a piece is fair."

Lieutenant Brant guffawed. "I was thinking closer to twenty-five cents each."

"Sir, you insult me." Annie's ma stamped her foot. "For that, I won't go below seventy-five cents apiece."

Lieutenant Brant looked over at his men and winked. He turned back to Annie's mother. "Thirty-five cents each."

She glared at him. "Fifty cents apiece, or you will leave my property *and* the rabbits!"

"You drive a hard bargain, Ma'am. Honestly, my men and I are only interested in the meat. If we leave you the pelts, can we cut that amount in half?"

"Now you are insulting me again."

"Sir," Private Wilkerson interjected. "I can make use of the pelts, with your permission, of course."

"Very well," said Lieutenant Brant with a sigh. He looked back at Annie's Ma. "Fifty cents, each?"

She nodded curtly.

The lieutenant reached into his pocketbook and pulled out the agreed-upon amount. Handing the notes to

Annie's Ma, he hesitated. "Could I have a few more moments of Annie's time?"

Ma blanched, and her voice caught in her throat. "For what purpose?"

The lieutenant shook his head. "Nothing nefarious, I assure you. We encountered a strange beast not far from here and I wanted to ask her if she has seen or heard anything out of the ordinary in recent days."

"There are many strange things in these woods." She shook her head. "Who knows what monsters the savages left behind when we moved onto their lands."

Lieutenant Brant nodded in understanding. "That may be so, but I would appreciate a few words with Annie, just the same."

"Annie!" Her ma yelled towards the house.

The wooden door creaked open as Annie peered out from behind it. Six other young faces looked at the grown-ups assembled in their yard.

"Yes, Ma?" Annie asked.

"The lieutenant has some questions for you. Come here."

"Coming, Ma." Annie shooed her siblings back into the house and walked slowly towards the adults.

"Hurry up now. They haven't got all day!" Her ma admonished.

Annie ducked her head and picked up her pace, closing the distance rapidly.

"Go ahead," her ma said to the lieutenant.

"Annie, when you found those rabbits, was there anything strange?"

"Strange how?"

"Anything out of the ordinary."

Annie looked at the lieutenant with knitted brows and her mouth drew into a thin line.

The lieutenant shook his head. "Let's try this. Can you describe the woods where you hunt?"

"No, Sir."

"Why not?" Lieutenant asked gently.

"I have a special spot in the woods where I find the best game. My snares are out there and everything. No offense, but I just met you today. How do I know you won't go to my spot and take my varmints?"

Lieutenant Brant chuckled. "I have no desire to steal your hunting grounds."

Annie crossed her arms and leaned back in disbelief.

"I'm asking what the woods are normally like. What are the sounds? What type of animals live there? That sort of thing."

Annie thought and looked to her ma. Her ma nodded and motioned for her to answer the lieutenant's questions.

"Well, Sir. I go out almost every morning, except Sundays of course."

Lieutenant Brant nodded in understanding.

"Can you tell me about the morning when you hunted those rabbits?" He pointed where Red and Cookie were processing the meat on the back of the wagon.

"It started out normal-like. I went to my spot, making sure to stay quiet. I learned a long time ago that if I'm too loud, I'll scare the game away."

"That makes sense. Go on."

"Well, it was quieter than usual that morning. Normally birds are chirping as they start their day. I thought it was extra quiet due to the fog, but it was too cold for fog. Winter just ended and that morning, the ground was frozen under my feet. I had to bust ice off the pump to prime the well for water. Too cold for fog like that." She looked away like she was putting herself back inside her hunting grounds.

"Anyway," she continued. "I managed to spot those rabbits and shot them real quick-like. I gathered them into my sack and started back for home."

"Was anything different about your walk home that morning?"

"Come to think of it, yes!" Her eyes widened and her words came out in a rush. "There are tons of critters in the woods all the time, but I always feel safe there. The animals who live there don't pay me too much mind, unless I make too much noise, of course."

"Of course. Please continue." The lieutenant made a motion with his hand for her to keep talking.

"Right. That morning, I felt like something was watching me. Something—big—I know not to run from dogs when they want to chase me, so I didn't run.. As I got closer to home, I heard branches crack behind me. I didn't turn around though, just kept my head high and kept up my brisk pace. I made it home and closed the door behind me when I got inside."

Annie's ma looked horrified. "Why didn't you say anything about this earlier?"

"I didn't want you to worry Ma. Besides, if you won't let me go hunt, who else is gonna hunt for meat?"

Annie's ma shook her head and tears started to form in her eyes. She pulled Annie into a hug and placed a kiss on top of her head.

"Do you have any more questions, Sir?" her ma asked.

"Only one. Other than the branch cracking, did you hear anything else?"

Annie pulled away from her ma's embrace and scrunched her face up while she thought.

"Actually, yes. I heard wolves howling in the distance."

"Is that normal for these parts?"

"Is it, but I don't ever hear anyone out here whistling."

# Chapter Four

The wagon creaked and groaned as it traversed the well-worn path through the woods. After hearing Annie's report of her experience on her hunt, the men were all deep in thought.

Red hung his head on the buckboard next to Cookie. The more he thought about his mare, the more upset he became. When the horses started to panic, he should have done more to calm them. If he had tied her halter tighter, she wouldn't have slipped out of it. If he had given her more forage, maybe she would still be a part of their mission, instead of…he couldn't finish the thought.

They trundled on towards Greenville when one of the horses pulling the wagon alerted. He stopped, his head lifted with pricked-up ears causing the other horse to stumble before halting as well. Cookie broke the silence, "What is it boy?"

Corporal Miller and Private Wilkerson rode up to find out why the wagon had stopped.

Cookie looked at the Corporal. "He just stopped. He must hear something we can't."

The mounted men placed their hands to their ears in a cupped shape. They strained and looked around, but there seemed to be nothing out there.

As they peered through the surrounding trees, a breeze picked up. The wind blew the branches and leaves in an erratic pattern that prevented the men from seeing beyond their immediate location.

Red shouted, "What is that?" He stood in the wagon and pointed to the west.

Thundering hoofbeats pounded the ground like drums and the men took aim with their rifles. The pounding grew louder as whatever it was neared them, but no shape resolved itself. Here they were, the sun bright in the sky overhead, but they were unable to see clearly through the persistent foliage.

Lieutenant Brant tensed and strained to hear over the coming stampede. Just as they were about to be overtaken, the sound ceased. His white knuckles turned back to pink as he relaxed his grip on the wooden stock of his rifle. He gazed warily around.

Corporal Miller and Private Wilkerson dismounted and handed their reins to Red as they patrolled a few meters around the wagon.

When everyone's breathing had mostly returned to normal, Wilkerson approached the Lieutenant. "Sir, we found something."

Lieutenant Brant nodded and followed Wilkerson through the scraggy underbrush. It snagged on his trousers and ripped a hole in his shirt, but he trudged on after the resolute private.

After about fifty yards, Private Wilkerson bent down.

The Lieutenant followed his gaze. He expected to see hoof prints, not whatever this abomination was. The print looked to belong to a man, but no human he knew had claws like a bear on his feet. *Just what are we dealing with out here?* he wondered silently. The depth of the print in the frozen mud suggested something much heavier than a man, even one carrying a rifle and pack. Lieutenant Brant shook his head and looked at Wilkerson.

"What is it, Sir?"

"I reckon I don't quite know. Never seen anything like it before."

Private Wilkerson took out a sketchpad and started to draw the print. He estimated the measurements and logged those as well. Once they reached Greenville, the lieutenant could send another message via telegram and add these details to his updated report.

His task completed, Wilkerson nodded to Lieutenant Brant, and they returned to the wagon.

Private Wilkerson looked up at the buckboard and frowned. "Where's Red?" he asked Cookie.

Cookie shrugged his beefy shoulders. "He was just here a moment ago." He jumped off the buckboard, much more nimbly than one would assume for a man of his girth and walked to the back of the wagon. After a few moments, he returned to Wilkerson and the Lieutenant. "There's no sign of him. It's like he just disappeared."

The private protested. "He wouldn't just wander off. That's not like him at all."

Lieutenant Brant placed a hand on Wilkerson's shoulder. "He was pretty broken up about losing his mare."

"I know, Sir, but he wouldn't run off and leave the rest of us like this. It just isn't in his nature."

The lieutenant shook his head. "Let's take a break for a quick supper. If he isn't back in an hour, we have no choice but to leave him behind."

"Sir, may I go look for him?" asked Wilkerson.

"Our party started out small to begin with. I'm afraid I have no one to spare to go with you, and I won't be losing any more of my men today." He gave the private a sharp look.

"What about Corporal—"

"Corporal Miller needs to rest as much as you do. Take a break son. I'm sure Private Flanagan is fine."

It was obvious Private Wilkerson didn't agree, but he wouldn't change the lieutenant's mind. In a small voice, he replied, "Yes, Sir."

The thundering of hooves grew louder and louder until Red could feel the pounding inside his very head. His brain bounced around inside his skull causing his eyes to bulge in time with the rhythmic beat.

Private Flanagan jumped off the buckboard and ran into the woods to put some distance between himself and the onslaught approaching them. He pressed the palms of his hands to his eyes to relieve some of the pressure but to no avail. Now his eardrums threatened to burst, leaving him unable to hear anything ever again.

Just as quickly as the stampede started, it just—stopped.

Red peeked around the trunk of a nearby tree and expected to see a war party riding astride painted ponies with muskets or spears pointed in his direction. Instead, he saw a lone horse, small and chestnut in color.

His breath caught in his chest. *I thought you were dead.*

His mare was there in a clearing grazing happily, flicking her ears, and swishing her tail at the few bugs who landed on her flank.

Red ran out to her with tears in his eyes. Suddenly a cloud of black smoke appeared between them. He coughed at the stench of decay that assaulted his nose. His throat became raw and scratchy and breathing became difficult. He tried to look past the cloud at his mare but could not see her through the tears in his eyes.

A voice emerged from the cloud, "This is your mount?"

"Yes," Red rasped through chapped lips. "I thought she was dead."

"She was."

The voice started to take shape. A man about ten feet tall towered over Red. His eyes glowed with a yellow eeriness and antlers sprouted from his head where his ears should be. Fingernails stretched into long talons that reached out and away from his looming frame.

Red stumbled backward, tripping over an exposed root.

He peered down at Red and stroked a claw along his jawline. "Your mount was dead, but I have the power to bring her back to you."

"Y-you can do that?" Red stammered.

The antlered man waved away Red's comment like he was swatting a mosquito. "I can do that and so much more. Would you like me to show you?"

Red looked from his mare, still grazing without a care in the world, to the strange man before him. "What will this cost me? I don't have any notes."

The man chuckled. "My payment does not require earthly currency. Simply agree to serve me, and the mare will be restored."

"That sounds simple enough…" Yet, Red hesitated.

"This will be much easier for you if you comply. I have ways to compel you into my service."

"Wait, what?"

The man moved with a swiftness that belied his towering bulk and came at Red with his talons. The wool of his uniform ripped and shredded along Red's chest, blood dripping down to his belt, staining the brass of his rectangular belt buckle.

Red gasped as his heart was pulled from his chest. He stood in a daze, the sound of thundering hoofbeats returning and surrounding him.

His mare looked at him then faded away, joining the man as he disappeared back into the cloud of smoke. He blinked once, yellow eyes glowing like a full moon.

Red looked down at his blood-covered chest. He pressed his hands where his heart once was and shuddered. Instead of warmth, his chest felt like the surface of the lake on Christmas Day. He pulled his hands away, but they stuck to his skin, ice shards tinkling to the frozen ground. *What did that creature do to me? And where is my mare? What have I done?* As his consciousness waned, the voice warned, "I will call you soon. When I do, you will answer."

The disembodied voice faded away, followed by whistling, a sound not unlike Red's pa calling to the family dog. Then Red heard no more.

# Chapter Five

"We can't wait any longer, Private! Mount up and let's get going." The Lieutenant was insistent.

Wilkerson knew he was right. He just couldn't shake the feeling that Red was in trouble. He had peeked around the perimeter of their impromptu rest spot without a sign of Red anywhere. There were no copper-colored hairs, no pieces of torn uniform stuck in the brambles, no boot prints, nothing. It was as if Red had just completely disappeared.

"Yes, Sir," Wilkerson relented. Corporal Miller gave him an encouraging nod and handed him the reins to Dawson's bridle. The private checked to make sure his cinch was tight, placed his left foot in the stirrup, and swung his right leg up and over his mount's back into the saddle.

He checked his seat, making sure his buttocks were not touching the cantle of his saddle. Stretching his legs, Private Wilkerson ensured his boots were on the tread of the stirrup, and his heels were down. He rolled his shoulders back and lifted his chin. After a moment, he was ready.

Dawson nickered his agreement and nibbled playfully at David's right boot.

Wilkerson chuckled. "I know boy, I'm ready to head back home, too." He rubbed his withers gently as they made their way down the bumpy trail.

Without Red's weight in the wagon, Cookie was able to drive the horses at a somewhat faster pace than earlier that morning. They picked up a brisk trot, nostrils wide, and warm breath exhaled like steam from the train that brought them to Ohio.

Wilkerson maintained his vigilance. Red could be out here anywhere. *Or whatever took him.* He shook his head. *There is no such thing as monsters.*

Corporal Miller rode Beau over to Dawson and spoke in a low voice. "Do you think Red deserted?"

"No. There is no chance of that."

"He was pretty broken up about what happened to his mare."

"Wouldn't you be if something like that happened to Beau?"

The corporal looked down between Beau's ears and patted his shoulder with his off-hand. "Yeah, I suppose I would."

Wilkerson nodded at the corporal, and they spent the rest of their trip in companionable silence.

The sun sat low on the horizon, peeking out behind the distant hills as they approached Greenville. Lieutenant Brant stopped and pulled out his map and compass.

Corporal Miller said to Wilkerson, "I don't know why, but seeing the lieutenant with a map makes me nervous."

Private Wilkerson looked at him blankly and shrugged.

The Corporal shook his head. "Never mind. Maybe when you become a corporal you will understand my unease."

"No offense, but I'll be relieved to make it to the end of this mission."

"Men! Gather 'round." The lieutenant beckoned them over to where he stood at the head of the column. He pointed down the trail, then down to the map. "If my compass bearings are accurate–" Corporal Miller gave Wilkerson a surreptitious glance "–we should make it to Greenville within the hour.

"On the off chance it should take longer, we should plan on making camp here for the night."

"Sir, if I may?" asked Cookie.

The lieutenant regarded their camp cook and supply sergeant. He looked a might disheveled with a three-day beard and coffee stains on the shirt he wore underneath his uniform. Despite the evening chill, his jacket was tied around his waist leaving his forearms bare to the icy air.

"What is it, Sergeant?"

"I cannot speak for the rest of our troop, but I would rather push it to Greenville than spend another night out in these Godforsaken woods!"

The honesty of Cookie's statement took the Lieutenant aback and he visibly recoiled as if slapped by the words.

Private Wilkerson added. "Sir, we already lost Red, and his horse out here. Do we want to risk losing anyone," he looked at the wagon, "or anything else?"

Lieutenant Brant looked from the private to Corporal Miller.

"Any sage words from my non-commissioned officer?"

"I agree with them, Sir. We should try to make it to town." He winked at Wilkerson. "And not just for the fine ladies no doubt waiting there to entertain us."

Lieutenant Brant shook his head. "Very well. I'm sure the horses would appreciate spending the night in a warm stable on a clean bed of straw, as opposed to tied to a rope and sleeping on their feet."

Dawson and Beau nickered as if they understood the Lieutenant's words.

"It's settled then. We continue on to Greenville."

He met each of the men's eyes as he continued. "If you see anything amiss, hear the slightest noise that seems out of place, get any inkling that makes your hackles stand up and salute, you will call a halt."

"Yes, Sir," they answered in unison.

"Move out!"

Thankfully, Lieutenant Brant's orienting skills were up to the task, and the troop made it into Greenville just as full dark settled along the square.

Corporal Miller and Private Wilkerson unsaddled Beau and Dawson, taking advantage of the stable's warmth. The boy working at the Livery protested, saying it was his job to feed and water the horses, but Miller and Wilkerson each handed him a three-cent nickel to look the other way.

"I promise not to tell your boss," said Wilkerson. "Besides, it is warmer in here than in the Wagner House," he added with a smirk. The Livery boy's eyes shrank from the size of saucers, and he nodded.

"Very well, Sir. You may not want to sleep out here though. Rats," he said the last with a whisper.

"Quite right," agreed Corporal Miller. "Besides I plan to spend my night in the arms of a beautiful woman."

"You might have better luck out here with the rats," said Wilkerson.

Corporal Miller spun around to face the private. "Was, was that a joke? I didn't think you were capable of humor."

"I can tell a joke," Wilkerson said defensively. "Red and I used to—" he hung his head at the thought of his missing friend.

The Corporal put his arm around his shoulder. "Come now, we'll find your friend. Or he'll find us. In any event, there are women, or in your case, whiskey waiting for us. Let's go!"

Private Wilkerson swatted the corporal's arm off his shoulder and followed him across the street.

# Chapter Six

Lively music reached them as they crossed the packed dirt road to the Wagner House. The proprietor wiped at the long wooden slab while filling mugs and glasses in between swipes. Beautiful ladies sat at a large round table looking at the patrons with sultry smiles and flattering eyes.

Corporal Miller pointed to a blond seated closest to the door. "That one reminds me of a gal I met on my first mission. I wonder if she has the same tricks…" He patted Private Wilkerson on the shoulder and made a beeline for the pretty young lady.

The private meandered through the crowd and bellied up to the bar. Looking at the various options, he remembered what the corporal had said. When the barkeep sauntered over, he placed his order. "Whiskey, please."

The barkeep nodded, revealing a bald spot on the top of his round head. The rest of his hair was dark brown and trimmed neatly around his ears. He had long sideburns that traced his jawline and ended just at either side of his chin. Rosy cheeks glowed beneath kind blue eyes that sparkled as he set the shot glass down on the bar.

"Thank you, Mister."

"*Bitte.*" The barkeep nodded again and went to check on the rest of his patrons.

Private Wilkerson couldn't recall the last time he had been in a tavern. That was probably because this was his first time inside of one. He grew up in a small town on the outskirts of Clear Creek and the neighbors didn't take kindly to drinking and carousing in public. There was no hotel or tavern there, only an addition to the home of the mayor, whose wife took pity on passersby and gave them a warm meal and a place to sleep while on their travels.

He took in the scene and smiled. Cookie was standing at the tall backed piano singing his lungs out. While making grub on the trail, Cookie had often hummed a tune or two to himself, but the men had never heard him sing before. His booming baritone carried throughout the room and those who knew the words instantly sang along. Private Wilkerson chuckled when Cookie waved him over. He shook his head and lifted his glass to his lips, draining the last drop of the whiskey and holding up the empty glass.

Cookie winked at him and turned his attention back to the pianist.

Lieutenant Brant walked up behind Wilkerson and waved the barkeep over.

"What can I do for you Sir?" the barkeep asked.

"Get this young man whatever he wants and add it to my tab. He's had a rough time of it, and I'd like him to enjoy his night off."

"Sir, I couldn't possibly—" Private Wilkerson protested.

Lieutenant Brant waved his comment away. "Think nothing of it, David. This mission was not what I, or anyone else, thought it would be." He scanned the room. "And I have a feeling, it isn't completely over, yet."

"What do you mean Sir?"

"You see those ladies over yonder?"

"The ones Corporal Miller is chatting with?"

"Yes, the same. Do you notice anything interesting about them?"

David Wilkerson looked at the table of beautiful ladies but didn't notice anything out of the ordinary.

"No, Sir. What am I missing?"

Lieutenant Brant pointed at a dark-haired lady wearing a bonnet who appeared older than the others. "The older one there, she has a book peeking out of her skirt pocket."

Wilkerson looked again and saw the corner of a small leather-bound tome. "I see it now, Sir."

The Lieutenant nodded. "Do you notice anything about what they are drinking?"

Wilkerson scanned the table and none of the ladies had whiskey or beer in front of them. The liquid they were drinking was clear, and a few had bubbles that danced in their glasses whenever they were raised to the ladies' lips.

"I think I understand, Sir. These ladies are having water or soda, not any type of libation."

"Correct," responded Lieutenant Brant. "I meant what I said about you having a night off; however, keep your wits about you in case this group of women is planning on causing our host any trouble. We don't want another New Vienna on our hands."

"No, Sir."

"Besides, with what we've encountered in the woods, our mission may yet change. They tend to do that, especially when you think they are completed."

Private Wilkerson opened his mouth, and the Lieutenant held a shot glass up in his face.

"Don't worry about that now. I mean it. Tonight, try and have a good time. We'll regroup in the morning."

"But Sir—"

"That's an order Private!" The Lieutenant said the last with a wink.

Private Wilkerson shook his head and downed the whiskey.

Corporal Miller let out a whoop and waved at the private, then led the beautiful blond lady upstairs. Wilkerson couldn't help but giggle.

The other ladies at the blond's table stood abruptly. The older woman wearing a bonnet's hip hit the wood and knocked her drink to the floor. Glass shattered causing the music to stop, and all eyes to drift towards them. The bonneted woman nearly slipped and fell in the puddle her spilled drink created.

Wilkerson rushed over and caught her arm before she could land on the hardwood floor. "Ma'am, are you alright?"

She sniffed at him. "How dare you touch me!"

"Excuse me, Ma'am?"

"You men are all the same. Have a couple drinks and think you can do whatever you want with a member of the female persuasion."

"Ma'am, that's not—"

"Sure, it's not! Look at your friend." She glared as her eyes followed Corporal Miller and the blond woman up the stairs. Turning back to Wilkerson, she continued, "Drink will be the downfall of this Country, you mark my words!"

Wilkerson looked to Lieutenant Brant for assistance.

"Ma'am, you're causing a scene. Perhaps, it is time for you to leave."

She turned her ire to the Lieutenant. "I'll show you a scene—"

"Prudence, let's go." Another woman from their table walked over and grasped her by the hand. She gently tugged her away from Brant and Wilkerson and led her to the door. "Come, ladies. It's time to go." The rest of them nodded solemnly and filed outside.

"Should we follow them, Sir?" Wilkerson asked the lieutenant. "To make certain they go home?"

"No, I think she made her point for tonight. No doubt they'll be back again though." He looked over at Cookie who nudged the pianist with his elbow. Once again, a lively tune filled the room.

"Enjoy the rest of the night, David."

"Yes, Sir."

After a couple more whiskeys, he was ready to call it a night. He made his way to Lieutenant Brant and asked, "Sir, is it alright if I go check on the horses before I turn in?"

"I'm sure the stable boy has them well in hand."

"I know Sir, I just want to be certain."

"Very well, but no sleeping out there." Lieutenant Brant laughed, his green eyes dancing with mirth.

"Yes, Sir." Wilkerson headed out the hotel door.

As soon as his face left the warmth and comfort of the dining room, a chill ran down his spine. He wrapped his arms across his chest and rubbed at the gooseflesh on his arms through the woolen sleeves. Each breath created a fog that obscured his vision just enough to make him look at the ground as he walked. He felt—something—and came to a stop.

No longer could he hear the music and merriment from the hotel. The street was deathly silent. No one walked along the road, nor along the boardwalks. There were no crickets, bats, nor any of the usual nocturnal sounds for this time of the evening.

He craned his head around to get a better view of his surroundings. There was simply nothing. It was as if he had walked out of the hotel and into an empty cave.

A gust of wind blew across his back causing the tamed goose pimples to reemerge along with the hackles on his neck. He turned slowly and lowered his arms to his sides, hovering over the revolvers in his belt.

From his left, he heard a horse whinny, but the stables were to his right. He turned toward the sound and the ground started to rumble. It was just like back in those cursed woods. Thundering hoofbeats pounded ever closer to him, but there was nothing he could see, except the dark of night.

He scanned the distance as the noise grew closer, but still could see nothing, except for his breath, and the low fog swirling around his ankles.

Taking purposeful strides, he hurried towards where the stables should be and kept his back against the building. He kept his gaze on the street, and in the direction of the stampede that should be upon him at any moment.

Just when the noise crescendoed over him and threatened to throw him to the ground, it stopped. He blinked to clear his vision but could still see nothing. Wilkerson held his hand in front of his face. Now that was visible. He wasn't blind, there was just nothing out on the street with him.

So why did he feel like he wasn't alone?

From behind the stable came a single horse. Hooves plodded along the earth beside the building and Private Wilkerson turned toward it. A small chestnut mare with a white blaze stood before him. She reached out with her muzzle and sniffed at his pockets in search of sugar cubes. *This horse looks just like Red's mare. But how?* He had been the one to find her remains in the forest. Unless it wasn't her in the forest after all...

His eyes started to fill with tears. What if he was wrong? What if Red's mare was hale and he told Red otherwise? Red was gone, and it was all his fault.

Wilkerson reached out to stroke the mare's forelock and his hand disappeared into a cloud of smoke. He recoiled and reached for one of his revolvers.

Where the mare had been, now stood Red, only different.

"Red? Is that you?"

Where Red had previously only stood about 5'5", this man was easily six feet tall. He looked gaunt, almost skeletal. Red had always been pale, but this figure looked to be knocking on death's door.

"David, it is me. How do I look?" Red held his arms out to the sides and turned in a slow circle to show off his new physique. As he finished the spin, his eyes met David's. There was no mistaking the mischief in those eyes. It was him alright.

"But, how? You disappeared. I searched for you. And how did you get so——?" Wilkerson waved his arm up and down in Red's direction.

"I got lost in the woods but was found. A new friend saved me and my mare. He can save you, too."

"What are you talking about? I don't need saving!"

"All men are evil and need to be saved. My new Master can show us the way."

"Have you gone mad? We don't need a Master. I already have a Savior, and I thought you did too!"

"What kind of Savior would take my mare from me? Leave me alone in the woods with my sorrow? When my Master found me, he took away all my pain and restored me."

"Restored you? Have you seen yourself? You were better before."

"Was I? I was always the smallest among us. The runt. Look at me! No one will ever call me a runt again!"

"No one called you a runt before! What are you talking about?"

"My Master has shown me the way. He even gave me back my mount. Come with me, and he will restore you too."

In the blink of an eye, Red reappeared astride his mare. Their eyes glowed yellow in the darkness and the fog thickened and rose up to Wilkerson's hips. He pressed his back against the stable in disbelief.

On one hand, he was relieved to see his friend. On the other, was this vision before him the same man that rode with him just a few days ago? He shook his head.

*No, this isn't right.* Nothing can bring an animal back from the dead, especially one that had been so thoroughly mutilated. There was evil in play here and he wanted no part of it.

"No."

"What do you mean 'no'?"

"I mean, no. I am not going anywhere with you. Take your mare and go back to your master. Leave me be."

"I'm afraid I can't do that."

"Yes, you can. Now go!" He shouted the last.

Red's eyes grew a brighter hue of yellow.

"Hey, Wilkerson! What is taking you so long out there?"

The private looked over to the balcony of the hotel, where a shirtless Corporal Miller waved to him. He looked back at Red, but he was gone. Gone too was the chill in the air, and the fog that had trapped him in place just a moment before.

"I'm coming. Be right there."

Private Wilkerson stood away from the stable wall and took a deep breath. He leaned forward, the weight of his head and the whole world, pushing him down toward the frozen earth. Shuddering, he shook his head and looked up at the sky. Bright stars shined down on him, casting the street with an eerie glare.

Next, he shook out his hands. His whole body trembled. After a few moments, the shock of what he had witnessed passed and he turned to the stable door. The wooden door felt warm to his touch, and he pulled it open slowly.

Musky horse and sweet hay greeted his nostrils, and he inhaled the comforting scents. He passed by the tack area where the warm leather had been freshly oiled and wiped down. He examined his saddle and found it in better shape than before this mission had begun.

Nodding, he approached Dawson who nickered in greeting.

His horse yawned, sticking out his tongue, and rolling his eyes backward. David patted his old friend on the forehead and stroked down his face absentmindedly. Dawson returned his affection by rubbing against his hand.

He patted him once more and then turned back to the door. Peering around it, he scanned the street for any sign of Red and his returned-from-the-dead mare. There was nothing. The silence from before was replaced with crickets and instead of a low fog, the street stood clear and barren.

*Monsters aren't real, so how can I explain what I saw? Red's mare disappeared in a cloud of smoke, then Red has a chat with me and wants me to join his new 'Master.'* He shook his head.

Wilkerson looked up to the balcony and saw Corporal Miller and the blond woman from earlier kissing. He chuckled nervously and thought, *I must have imbibed too much whiskey. Everything appears back to normal now.*

He closed the stable door behind him, and with one more glance down the street crossed into the warmth and comfort of the hotel.

# Chapter Seven

"Wake up sleepyhead. We have new orders!" Private Wilkerson groaned at the assault to his senses. When he had returned from the stables last night, he partook of another couple of whiskeys to help calm his nerves so he could sleep. That had been a mistake.

Staggering to the wash basin, he splashed cold water on his face and dressed quickly after using the facilities.

Wilkerson tromped down the stairs and into the throng of activity at the bar.

"I trust you slept well," teased the Lieutenant.

"Sorry, Sir. It was a strange night."

Corporal Miller walked over. "Who were you talking to last night?"

"What do you mean? You saw him?"

"Saw who?" asked the corporal and lieutenant in unison.

*Maybe I wasn't imagining things,* Private Wilkerson thought. "Red! And his mare!"

"How much did you have to drink?" asked Corporal Miller.

"Not so much as to lose my mind," Private Wilkerson retorted. *Or is that what happened?*

The lieutenant looked solemn. "Start at the beginning."

Wilkerson gulped and told them everything that transpired in the street the previous night.

Cookie sighed. "I was afraid of that."

"Afraid of what?"

"I told you those woods was cursed? Now that demon done followed us!"

"There is no such things as demons," said Corporal Miller.

The lieutenant looked at him sternly. "Don't be so certain."

"Sir?" asked Private Wilkerson.

Lieutenant Brant sighed. "Men, we have new orders, and I don't think you are going to like them."

Corporal Miller said, "That is why they are called 'orders' right Sir?"

The lieutenant sighed again. "Be that as it may. We have to go back into the woods and return to the camp."

Cookie blanched. "Why Sir?"

Lieutenant Brant roared, "Who am I to question our orders?" A vein in his forehead bulged and his face turned beet red.

The men stared at him. They had never seen him so upset before.

The lieutenant took a deep calming breath, met each of his men's eyes, and continued.

"Now then. Our orders are to return to the camp. Since we left, there have been more strange occurrences happening."

"You don't say," Cookie mumbled under his breath.

The lieutenant raised his eyebrows at him.

Cookie ducked his head in shame.

"Apparently, farm animals have been massacred, with only bones and bits of flesh left behind. The people who live in the woods are concerned, especially coming out of a long hard winter."

"Sir," said Corporal Miller. "That sounds suspiciously like the state we found Red's mare in." He gulped and looked at Private Wilkerson.

Private Wilkerson went pale. "How many animals have they found like that?" he asked the lieutenant.

"Enough to have called us for reinforcements."

"I thought we were here to keep tabs on the ladies," said the corporal.

"And I'm certain you enjoyed your mission with your blond friend last night," replied the Lieutenant. "As I said to Wilkerson, missions tend to change. Instead of babysitting a few teetotalers, we now need to go back into the woods to discover who, or what, is attacking the livestock."

Cookie cleared his throat. "Don't they have a Sheriff or a Marshal who can help them? How is this within our purview?"

Lieutenant Brant shook his head. "The Law is worn thin in these parts. They have to keep tabs on the local rabble-rousers as well as maintain their jail facilities. When something like this comes along, they don't have the resources to handle it. We do."

"Do we, Sir?" asked Private Wilkerson. "Not to question orders, but how are we equipped to deal with something like I encountered last night?"

"Our trip to the general store wasn't only for the items on the manifest." Lieutenant Brant looked sternly at his gathered men. "What I am about to share with you is most secret. Our mission is to hold the line."

"Yes, Sir, but against what, exactly?" asked Corporal Miller.

"We hold the line, between Heaven and Hell."

"'Heaven and Hell…,' Sir?" Private Wilkerson shifted in his chair.

"You heard me right. Our troop is part of an elite force within the United States Army. What I am about to tell you does not leave this room. Do you understand?" The lieutenant met their gazes and continued.

"A Special Unit was formed when monsters of myth and legend started appearing within our world. The violence of war thinned the veil between their dimension and ours. Some of them came through.

"Over time, we have managed to send most of them back where they belong, but a few have eluded us. Still, others poke holes in the veil and come back through occasionally.

"I won't lie to you. This mission will not be easy. I still don't know exactly what we're dealing with, but I have help coming. He should arrive tomorrow and then we will venture boldly back through those woods and render aid.

"Any questions?"

Cookie and Private Wilkerson exchanged a glance. "Sir, what are our new orders? What about the temperance movement here in town?"

Lieutenant Brant placed his hand on Private Wilkerson's shoulder. "Our orders are to find and eradicate the beast plaguing the nearby woods. That is now our primary mission. People's lives are at stake, whether the beast attacks them directly, or not. Each time it kills an animal, it is robbing the people of their food source; that is just as bad as killing them outright. Without food, they will starve to death."

Cookie nodded. "That isn't how I would want to go." He patted his belly. "Speaking of, where is breakfast?"

Just then, a pretty serving girl with long brown hair brought out plates for the men. She reached in front of Private Wilkerson and knocked over his coffee cup. Blushing, she said, "I am so sorry. Let me get you a fresh cup."

The private looked into her brown eyes and his heart fluttered. "Not a problem, Miss." He used his napkin to mop up the puddle on the table.

The girl sighed. "I'm so clumsy…"

"Really, it's alright." Private Wilkerson accidentally touched her elbow with his napkin. Her face turned a deeper shade of red and she ducked away and bolted for the kitchen.

Cookie guffawed. "You sure have a way with the ladies, private."

It was Wilkerson's turn to blush.

Corporal Miller looked deep in thought. "You said we move out tomorrow, Sir?"

"That is correct."

"Very well then. If this is to be my last day on this Earth, I plan to enjoy it to the fullest." He winked at his blond companion from yesterday. "If you need me, I'll be in my bunk."

The serving girl returned with a fresh coffee for Wilkerson. "Can I get you anything else?"

Cookie dove into his food and grunted in the negative.

"I'm alright. Thank you, Miss." Wilkerson's voice cracked.

She gave him a shy smile and departed back to the kitchen.

Lieutenant Brant picked up a piece of bacon. "Private, when you and Cookie are done eating, tend to the horses and verify the wagon is ready for travel."

"I know my job, Sir." Cookie protested.

"Yes, and you try to do too much without asking for help. Let Wilkerson assist you. That's an order."

Cookie grumbled again.

The next morning, Private Wilkerson was the first man downstairs. Dawn peeked over the distant hills and cast a warm glow throughout the main floor of the Wagner House. He made his way to the kitchen, following the alluring aroma of coffee.

"Morning." He announced his presence at the threshold.

"*Guten Morgan.*" Herr Wagner pointed to the coffee pot. "Help yourself to a fresh brew. I figured you boys would need it good and strong considering where you're headed."

"How do you know about our mission?"

"I don't, but I have heard stories about those woods. Why do you think I stay here in the hotel?" He turned back to the stove, stirring a cast iron pan filled with sausage gravy.

David pulled up a stool and inhaled deeply. The last time he had a home-cooked meal was before he shipped out. Cookie was no slouch when it came to reheating provisions and adding spices, but meals out of a can warmed over a campfire left much to be desired, especially when they had been out in the field for so long.

"Do I smell biscuits?" Cookie rounded the corner and plopped down next to Wilkerson. "Mmm, that smells heavenly."

Herr Wagner smiled. "Almost ready boys. Head on out to the dining room. I'll be along shortly."

They thanked him and grabbed a table in the far corner, away from the front door and any early morning visitors.

Sipping the piping hot coffee, they sat in companionable silence. Cookie's stomach rumbled causing David to laugh. It was just what he needed to break the building tension.

Herr Wagner brought out the food. A vat of gravy was surrounded by a basket of fresh biscuits, butter, scrambled eggs, and a pile of bacon as big as his head. He set down plates and utensils just in time for Lieutenant Brant and Corporal Miller to join them.

Private Wilkerson noticed an extra plate on the table. "Will you be joining us?" he asked their host.

The front door creaked open, and all the men tensed. Sergeant Taylor reached for his revolver with his right hand – his left was busy with four strips of greasy bacon.

The lieutenant stood and motioned the troop to relax. He went to greet the newcomer.

A man of average height with tanned skin, and dark brown hair approached the lieutenant and offered his hand. He wore a breechclout over a pair of deerskin leggings. Moccasins adorned his feet. About his head, he wore a colorful scarf. They gripped forearms in the warriors' style and spoke in hushed voices.

Wilkerson couldn't make out their words. He strained to listen, then remembered what his Ma had taught him. *It isn't polite to eavesdrop.*

He shook his head and shoveled a spoonful of scrambled eggs into his mouth.

Cookie grinned at him, a dribble of gravy working its way down his whiskers.

Corporal Miller just stared at the man. He seemed more intense than usual, and Wilkerson thought he knew why.

The lieutenant was conversing with a Savage. One of the Natives that had brought so much death and destruction to their people back before the Civil War. Many settlers had lost their homes, and their lives, fighting to make a life for themselves and future generations.

The Natives hadn't taken kindly to the encroachment by the settlers and went to war for many decades.

Now that the War was over, each side picked up the pieces as best they could. The Union was reunited – mostly – and life was starting to get back to normal. The Natives had their allotted grounds, and the settlers were able to continue to clear land and plant farms in relative peace.

Still, some could not forgive the Natives for the atrocities they committed in decades past. It seemed Corporal Miller was one of those men. He started to rise from the table and Wilkerson placed a hand on his elbow.

"What are you doing, *Private?*"

"Lieutenant Brant knows what he is doing. Trust him."

Miller flopped back into his seat and tore a chunk from a freshly buttered biscuit. "We'll see," he grumbled as crumbs flew out of his mouth.

Lieutenant Brant and his companion approached the table. Wilkerson could see the Native in more detail now. He had a ring inserted in the columella of his pronounced nose. His hair hung loose over his shoulders. Bright black eyes scanned the men, and he huffed in disapproval.

"What is the matter?" Lieutenant Brant asked him.

"These men are soft. They know not what waits for them."

Private Wilkerson looked up into his eyes. He saw determination there, without a hint of fear. This man had seen much and lived through it.

The lieutenant pointed to a chair and the man sat, keeping his hands visible to the rest of the troop.

Wilkerson noticed a tomahawk strapped to his back and two hunting knives in leather holsters at his hips. He looked at the man and then down at his plate when he realized he was staring.

The Native spoke again. "This one," he said pointing to Wilkerson, "has seen the darkness."

David's blood ran cold, and he dropped the fork filled with eggs and gravy to his plate with a clatter.

The man stared at Wilkerson then tucked his head to his chest and closed his eyes.

Everyone at the table grew silent. All that could be heard were the sounds of Herr Wagner in the kitchen stirring the gravy and pulling another batch of biscuits out of the oven.

After a few moments, the man looked up and pierced David with his stare.

"Tell me what you saw."

Private Wilkerson looked at the lieutenant who gave him a stern nod. He took a deep breath and recounted his vision of Red and his mare. After he was done, the man closed his eyes again.

David opened his mouth to speak, but the lieutenant stopped him with a shake of his head. He leaned over to Wilkerson and whispered, "This is part of his process. Just be patient."

"Yes, Sir," David whispered back.

Corporal Miller just rolled his eyes and poured himself another mug of coffee while Cookie continued shoveling food into his portly face.

After what felt like an eternity, the Native spoke. "I have consulted with the spirits."

Miller let out a guffaw.

The lieutenant snapped his fingers in Miller's face, who ducked his head.

"They say you are dealing with a Stonecoat."

"What's that?" asked Wilkerson.

"I told you those woods were cursed," said Cookie through a mouthful of biscuit.

"A Stonecoat is a creature that used to be a man. Once he has consumed human flesh, the Wendigo Spirit lives inside him and transforms him into an evil monster."

"What do they look like?" asked David, enthralled.

"The most common form is of a large skinny man with antlers like a buck. They have long talons on their fingers like an eagle and claws on their feet like a bear. Also, their eyes glow pale yellow like milk that has gone sour."

David went pale again. "Sir, when I saw Red, his eyes glowed like the full moon."

The Native nodded. "The spirits are never wrong."

"Oh, come on!" roared the corporal. "Sir, you can't possibly believe this hill of beans."

"Corporal, Silent Owl has been an asset of my special unit for some time. He knows these woods and the local lore. Also, he is a tracker and can help us find and put an end to this Stonecoat."

Silent Owl nodded. "What he says is true." He looked at the food and the lieutenant nodded. He helped himself to a mug of coffee and two strips of bacon.

Wilkerson had so many questions. How were they supposed to find, much less fight, a Stonecoat? Since when were monsters real? And, what about Red? His heart started to hammer in his chest. The delicious food threatened to crawl its way out of his throat due to the butterflies in his stomach pushing it out and up. He swallowed and took a deep breath.

Lieutenant Brant looked over at him. "You alright there, Private?"

He shook his head, thought better of it, then nodded. "I will be, Sir."

Silent Owl watched him but said nothing.

"I still say this is a bad idea." Corporal Miller was sore about having a Native join their mission.

"I have registered your complaint, *Corporal.* That will be enough." Lieutenant Brant made his decision clear. Silent Owl was coming with them, and that was that.

Cookie rode on the buckboard, leather driving reins in his hands as he deftly maneuvered the wagon down the trail back into the woods.

Silent Owl rode up to Wilkerson on his war pony. The mare was small, maybe only fourteen hands with a chestnut coat and white blotches along her neck and rump. Three of her legs were white, and her other markings were a star on her forehead and a white snip on her muzzle beneath her left nostril. As small as the war pony was, she easily kept pace with Dawson and Beau who plodded down the well-worn trail. Compared with their last trip along this stretch, both geldings were relaxed and reached for the grasses poking through the melting snow as they walked.

Silent Owl leaned over his pony's withers and spoke in a low voice. "Do you remember where your friend's mare ran off?"

"Yes, Sir, can I call you Sir?"

Silent Owl made a low sound almost like a cat purring. "You may refer to me as Shaman. I speak with the spirits and help my tribe when people are ill or injured."

"Yes, Shaman. We made camp a few hours from here. Whatever that beast was attacked us shortly after nightfall. We found the mare's remains the next morning."

"Hmph," he intoned. Without another word, he rode up to the lieutenant and they spoke in hushed voices.

It was the corporal's turn to whisper to David. "Why do they keep whispering? What secrets are they keeping up there?"

"Probably deciding when they are going to scalp you."

Corporal Miller took a double-take. "Was that another joke?"

Wilkerson chuckled. "You should see the expression on your face."

"Why would you say something like that?"

"Why are you so afraid of him?" Private Wilkerson indicated the shaman.

"Let's just say I have my reasons." With that, he squeezed Beau with his calves and moved up the line closer to the lieutenant who rode point.

David took in his surroundings. Without the dank fog and absence of sound, it was a rather lovely trail through the forest. Birds chirped happily in the tree canopy. Warm sunlight lay across his shoulders like a fleece blanket and a pleasant breeze wafted around him.

He took a deep breath and enjoyed the scent of pine needles and maple in the air. With the coming spring, new life started to emerge in the forest, the harshness of winter well behind them. The frozen ground thawed under Dawson's hooves, and they made their way quietly to the campsite without incident.

# Chapter Eight

As dusk settled upon the clearing, Cookie prepped the camp. The men unsaddled and brushed down their horses making use of the highline they used a few days before.

Wilkerson unloaded a bale of hay and a bag of oats from the wagon to feed the geldings after taking them for a drink in the nearby creek.

Supper was nothing to write home about: a can of beans, some canned ham, and cream corn. Cookie's spices helped make it more palatable, but it tasted nothing like the breakfast they had enjoyed that morning.

After eating his fill, David wrapped his blanket around him, laid his head on his saddle and closed his eyes.

No sooner did his vision go dark, hoofbeats thundered in the distance. *Not this again!*

He rose from his makeshift bed and grabbed his Henry rifle. The campfire still glowed in the center of the clearing and the rest of the men were nowhere to be found. He scanned the highline and the horses were gone, as well.

Wilkerson's heart rate quickened, and his eyes grew wide. His chest grew tight as he strained to breathe. A fog emerged from his mouth, clouding his vision, and causing his eyes to water. Sweat dampened his palms, making it difficult to keep his grip on the rifle.

He pulled his left hand away from the stock and wiped it on his trousers. Keeping his right finger away from the trigger, he pointed the muzzle towards the incoming stampede.

The fire grew brighter, flames rising into the air, sparks dancing in the darkness and filling the space with an orange glow.

As David watched the flames, a form took shape. The smoke coalesced and red coals gleamed from within. A man with antlers where his ears should be walked through the flames towards him.

He wore a dark cloak that protected him from the heat of the fire. Stalking closer, the man opened his mouth. "It is time for you to choose."

"Choose what?" Wilkerson screamed at the man. Confusion made his head hurt. He just wanted to find Red, finish this mission, and go home.

"Join us, or die!"

The man opened his arms and within the cloak was another form. A smaller man with red hair and freckles along his nose and cheek walked out of the fire. Red stood before David and beckoned him forward.

"No!" David screamed. "I will never join you!"

"You had your chance," the man with antlers spoke, but the words sounded inside Wilkerson's mind.

The fire grew as the man disappeared, taking Red with him. Flames licked out of the fire pit, embers spreading around the camp and setting the nearby brush ablaze. Wilkerson tried to put the fires out, but the flames grew in intensity. He coughed, smoke violating his lungs, making it impossible to breathe.

Suddenly he felt a hand on his chest. He looked to his right and saw Silent Owl. "Come with me if you want to live."

David was perplexed. *What was happening?*

"The spirits are with you. Take my hand."

Wilkerson reached his shaking hand hesitantly and grasped Shaman's outstretched one.

He sat up, the morning light filling the camp with warmth and comfort.

David looked around and saw the horses grazing peacefully along the highline. The men gathered around the firepit, a coffee pot set on top of the coals.

Shaman looked at him. "You have been marked."

"Was I dreaming?"

"Yes, and no."

"What does that mean?"

Lieutenant Brant walked up to them. "How did you sleep?"

"Sleep? I was asleep?"

The lieutenant and Shaman exchanged a glance.

"Gather your men. This is more serious than I feared."

"Fill your coffee and come here," Lieutenant Brant shouted to make sure everyone heard him.

Wilkerson staggered to the fire and Cookie handed him a steaming mug. He held it in both hands, allowing the heat to warm his frozen fingers. He blew on the surface of the coffee and raised it to his trembling lips.

Shaman spoke. "We were attacked last night."

Corporal Miller guffawed. "Attacked? I slept like a baby."

Cookie looked at him and shook his head. "I told you these woods are cursed."

"Not exactly," said Silent Owl. "The spirits showed me there is an evil here. David saw it, too."

Everyone turned to Private Wilkerson who gave them a sheepish grin. "I saw Red again."

"Red? He's alive?" asked the corporal.

"I think so, but I can't be certain."

"Your friend is under the influence of a malevolent power," Shaman said. "It is using him to take David. The young private and I fought them, but they will keep trying."

"How did we fight them? I just waved my rifle around and took your hand when you told me to."

"Remember, the spirits are with you." Silent Owl smiled. "The danger has not passed. We are safe in the daylight, but come nightfall, we need to be out of these woods."

The lieutenant pulled out his map. "We should make it to North Star before noon, if we leave soon."

Corporal Miller chuckled, "The lieutenant and his map again."

Private Wilkerson just rolled his eyes. He finished his coffee and approached Shaman. "Why does Red keep coming after me?"

"You were friends?"

"I thought we were, but why would he try to conscript me into his master's service?"

"Perhaps, he is hoping you will save him. By reaching out to you, he wants to be free of his shackles. The Stonecoat will not let him go easily."

"How do we stop it?"

"There are many ways but let us start here." Shaman pulled something out of his pack. A small disk of obsidian spun underneath a leather cord. He bowed his head over it then slipped it over David's neck. "This will protect you."

"Protect me from what?"

Shaman winked at him. "The spirits are with you."

# Chapter Nine

As the men cleaned up their breakfast, Silent Owl walked over to Lieutenant Brant. Once again, they spoke in hushed voices. Wilkerson couldn't help but notice Shaman pointing at him as they spoke.

After a few minutes, the lieutenant came over by the fire. He sat down next to David and leaned over to speak in his ear. "Silent Owl says the Stonecoat is tracking you."

"Yes, Sir." Wilkerson sighed.

"This could be good news."

"How do you figure?"

"Instead of us going deeper into the woods to find it, we can wait for it to come to us."

"Are you suggesting using me as bait, Sir?" Wilkerson gulped, the saliva in his throat getting stuck halfway down his esophagus.

"No, Son. But if it comes to us, we can set an ambush."

"What about the rest of the town?"

"If Silent Owl is correct, and I believe he is, the Stonecoat will wait until nightfall to strike. We will have the rest of the men set a watch around the town, and make sure the civilians stay in their homes."

"That's not much of a plan, Sir."

"Not yet, but I will keep thinking on the way back to Greenville."

The trip back to Greenville was without incident. Maybe the spirits were looking out for them, after all.

Wilkerson walked Dawson in front of the mercantile and tied him to the hitching post.

Corporal Miller did the same with Beau.

They both looked up at the sound of the bell tinkling from the storefront.

Samson ran out to them, out of breath, and with a worried look on his face. "I am so relieved to see you."

"What has happened?" asked the corporal.

"Mr. Katzenberger still has not returned. After you took Miss Annie home, I thought he would be back any moment. I haven't seen hide nor hair of him since you left."

"It's only been a few days. Is that unusual?" asked the lieutenant as he entered their conversation.

"Quite," said Samson. "I am concerned something may have happened to him."

"Do you know where he went?" asked Lieutenant Brant.

"No, Sir, he just vanished when I was done checking to make sure your supplies were in order. This is quite unlike him. I've never managed the store by my lonesome!"

Shaman approached the distraught man. "Has he ever left for an extended period of time before now?"

Samson took a double take at the Native and looked to the lieutenant for guidance.

"He is with us. Please answer his question."

"No, not ever. This store is everything to him. I have worked for him for over five years and the only time he has taken leave was when the milk sickness got him back in the summer of '68."

He hung his head and grasped his face with his hands.

"Where does he live?" asked Silent Owl.

"Let me close the shop and I will show you." Samson went inside and turned the sign in the door to 'Closed.' He grabbed his traveling cloak and locked the front door behind him.

"It's a bit of a hike from here. Should we take the wagon?" Samson asked the lieutenant.

"I'd rather the wagon say here." The lieutenant crossed his arms. "Corporal Miller, let Samson borrow your mount."

"But, Sir," he protested. "Beau doesn't like just anybody riding him."

"I know that, but he is more docile than Dawson. Besides, I need you to stay here with Cookie and ask around if anyone has seen anything strange."

"Yes, Sir," Corporal Miller relented and led Beau up to the sidewalk.

"Wilkerson, I need you and Silent Owl to go with Samson. Report back here as soon as you are able."

"Yes, Sir." David mounted Dawson and followed Beau, with Samson astride, and Shaman's war pony out of town.

They meandered down a dark and overgrown trail on the south side of town. Despite the afternoon hour, sunlight didn't reach them below the overgrown canopy.

Silent Owl pulled his pony to a halt and peered ahead into the darkness. He dismounted and walked over to Samson. "Something here is wrong."

"Wrong how?" asked the shop owner's assistant.

"Don't you feel that?"

"Feel what?" he shrugged in Beau's saddle, oblivious to what the shaman meant.

Beau started to prance. He tossed his head and tried to turn back towards town.

Dawson picked up on Beau's nervousness and sidestepped closer to his herd mate.

Private Wilkerson dismounted. "Easy, Boy. You're alright." He handed his reins to Samson. "Stay here with the horses. If they bolt, head back to town and we will catch up."

Samson nodded.

Silent Owl leaned into Wilkerson. "Do you feel it?"

"I feel something, but I don't know what it is."

"The spirits are with you."

"You keep saying that."

Silent Owl grunted, then led David further into the dark.

After they cleared the thickest of the underbrush, they came upon a small clearing with a shack off to one side. Moss grew on the exterior walls and along the roof line. Vines crisscrossed over what appeared to be windows and sprouted along the uneven ground. Weeds covered the walkway and stretched as high as Wilkerson's hips.

"This doesn't look like the home of a merchant to me."

Shaman just grunted again, but he pulled his knives from his waist and placed one in his teeth, the other he held out in front of him.

"Do you see anything?"

"No," Silent Owl muttered around the blade, "but pay more attention to what you hear."

Private Wilkerson listened intently but didn't hear a thing. The entire clearing was devoid of sound, light, everything.

"I don't hear anything." David said to Shaman.

"Exactly, now be quiet."

Wilkerson nodded and followed Shaman around the back of the shack. The Native stayed low to the ground, prowling along the side of the building, head up and eyes alert.

The Private did his best to emulate Shaman but his training was nothing compared to a lifelong warrior. His boot came down on a twig and a loud *snap* pierced the stillness.

Silent Owl sighed and looked back at David, disappointment obvious on his face. He shushed him and kept moving.

As they rounded the back of the shack, the stench of copper assaulted them. Wilkerson made the mistake of taking a deep breath to calm his nerves and ended up gagging instead. He heaved and wretched into the bushes underneath the shattered pane set into a decrepit wall.

Silent Owl closed his eyes, listening for any sign of what may have caused the massacre before them. He gathered his composure and entered the shack through the back door.

Wilkerson followed him after wiping his mouth with his shirt sleeve and pulling his collar up over his nose and mouth to prevent smelling more of the carnage.

As he crossed the threshold, the interior of the shack was even more devoid of light than the outside woods. His eyes took a moment to adjust, then he saw Shaman with his head bowed, arms crossed over his chest, with his hands on the opposite shoulders.

"What are you doing?" he whispered.

"Asking forgiveness."

"Forgiveness for what?"

"Disturbing the final resting place of these people."

"What people?" David looked down at the floor and realization smacked him in the face. The blood they smelled had to come from somewhere, and now he saw the sources of it. Bodies in various stages of decomposition lay strewn across the floor. Most of them were only skeletons, but a few still had ragged strips of flesh determinedly hanging on to the bones. Skulls with empty eye sockets stared mockingly at the ceiling, the lids long ago eaten away by a beast or by nature. Wilkerson knew not which.

"Let's go, Shaman. Mr. Katzenberger isn't here."

Silent Owl grunted in assent. He bowed once more over the remains inside the cabin and followed David back to the trail where Samson and the horses waited.

"Did you find him?" asked Samson.

Wilkerson looked up at him and in a hoarse whisper answered, "Who were we supposed to find here?"

"Mr. Katzenberger. This is his cabin."

"I find that hard to believe. This 'cabin' as you call it is nothing more than a dilapidated old shack. I wouldn't let my dog live there, much less a man. Are you certain this is where the Mercantile owner lives?"

"Shack? What do you mean? Mr. Katzenberger has one of the nicest homes in these parts."

Silent Owl entered the conversation. "Are you certain you brought us to the correct place?"

"Yes, why?"

David shook his head. "Because this place is not the home of a shopkeeper, or anyone, at least not recently."

"What do you mean?"

"Currently, it is nothing but a boneyard."

"A boneyard? What are you talking about?"

Wilkerson pulled Samson out of the saddle and forced him toward the shack. "Does this look like Mr. Katzenberger's house to you?"

Samson stopped halfway to the shack and bent over. With his hands on his knees, he took a deep breath. "I swear this was his home. Last Christmas he invited me to dinner. I was certain this was the right place."

Silent Owl looked at Wilkerson and shook his head.

"And now that you've seen it?"

"No. I'm sorry. I must have taken a wrong turn somewhere. My apologies for wasting your time."

Wilkerson glared at him.

"Maybe? Yes! We can head back towards town and then take the other trail that follows the creek. I'm certain his home is out that way."

"You said you were certain about this place." Shaman kept his hand on the hilt of his knife.

Samson's eyes grew wide.

"It's starting to get late. We should head back to town, and we can try again tomorrow." Wilkerson stalked back to the horses.

As Samson approached, Beau snorted.

Wilkerson tapped him on the shoulder. "Knock it off. You'll see Corporal Miller soon enough."

Beau pinned his ears back and bared his teeth.

Silent Owl breathed into Beau's nostrils and he whickered softly.

Wilkerson held the reins as Samson mounted.

"I told you there is something wrong with that man." Shaman stared at Samson's back as they rode out of the woods.

They rode back into town in silence. Private Wilkerson could tell Silent Owl wanted to talk to him, but something about Samson made him hold his tongue. They approached the mercantile, dismounted, and tied their mounts to the hitching post.

David walked up to Samson. "Do you have any other ideas of where Mr. Katzenberger might be?"

"No, I do not. That is why I offered to take you to his home. Again, I apologize that I could not remember exactly where it is."

"I'm sure he'll turn up."

Samson nodded and checked the door of the mercantile to make certain it was locked.

Silent Owl approached Wilkerson. "There is something wrong about that man."

"Wrong how?"

"Did you notice how Beau acted when we got close to the shack?"

"I was nervous in that clearing myself." Wilkerson shuddered.

"Yes, but he would not let Samson get in the saddle."

Wilkerson shrugged. "Beau is particular about who rides him."

"It is more than that. Even the horses can sense he walks the path between two worlds."

"How is that possible?"

"Legend of the Stonecoat speaks about men who are consumed by the sickness. They try to remain amongst our world, but the evil chases them into the darkness of the other realm."

"What other realm?"

"The realm where the wendigo spirit lives."

"How can a man walk between worlds?"

"I know not, only what Legend says."

"Perhaps, you need to speak with the rest of the troop about this Legend."

"Mmm, perhaps."

Wilkerson untied Dawson from the hitching post. "Let's get the horses squared away and then find the rest of the men."

Silent Owl led his war pony and Beau to the livery.

They untacked the horses and made sure they had plenty of fresh hay and water. David brushed down Dawson, then Beau. He went to brush Shaman's pony, but Silent Owl stopped him.

"I will tend to my own horse."

"Alright." He handed him the brush and sat down on a nearby bale of hay.

Thinking on what he had just seen in that shack sent shivers down his spine. What kind of monster could do such a thing? What had those poor people done to deserve to be eaten and then left in a pile of bones? It made him sick to his stomach. The more he thought about it, the more bile started to crawl up his throat.

He ran outside and heaved into the street. The contents of his stomach had been left out by that shack, so all he had left was phlegm and bile. He gave all of it up and said a prayer once he was finished.

*Dear Lord, by all that is Holy, help me to find the creature responsible for these atrocities and put an end to it.*

*Help me to find Red and save him from a similar fate.*

*In Jesus' name. Amen.*

He turned back to the livery and saw Silent Owl watching him from the doorway.

"Come," he said. "You look like you could use some whiskey."

# Chapter Ten

Wilkerson and Shaman entered the tavern to find the rest of the troop huddled around a large wooden table at the back corner of the dining room. An empty bottle of whiskey lay in the middle of the table surrounded by shot glasses.

"Looks like they started without us." David chuckled.

Shaman walked up to the lieutenant. "May we join you?"

The lieutenant pulled out a chair. "Sit, we have much to discuss."

The serving girl from earlier made her way over with a fresh bottle and two more glasses for the new arrivals. She placed the glasses down, poured them full to the brim, and gave Wilkerson a shy smile.

David and Shaman sat, and each reached for a glass.

"Wait," said the lieutenant. "First, we toast."

He filled the others' glasses and each of the men reached in.

Holding his glass up in the air, the others followed suit. "To holding the line…"

"Between Heaven and Hell!" The rest of them chorused, then threw back their drinks.

A comforting burn filled David's belly and he reached to refill his glass.

Shaman placed a hand on his elbow. "Better to keep a clear head for what I have to share with you."

Wilkerson nodded and placed his hands together on the table, folded in prayer.

Shaman made an approving sound deep in his throat.

"Ok, boys." Lieutenant Brant spoke. "Tell us what you found out there."

Shaman raised an eyebrow at David indicating for him to start.

Private Wilkerson took a deep breath and started at the beginning.

When he was done, he looked to Shaman. "Am I forgetting anything?"

Silent Owl grunted. "No, but I have some things to add."

The lieutenant peered at him from across the table. "Are we dealing with a Stonecoat or something else?"

"Yes, I believe so, but something more, also."

Corporal Miller snorted. "A Stonecoat wasn't enough. Now we have to fight two demonic monsters?"

Wilkerson interjected. "There is no such thing as demons."

Lieutenant Brant shook his head. "After everything you've seen, you still doubt what we have to do?"

"No, Sir. I don't doubt our mission. I believe there is evil in this world, and I understand it is our job to eradicate it. What I question is whether the evil is from a demonic source, or simply from the Devil."

Corporal Miller waved his arms in frustration. "Demons? The Devil? What does it matter?"

"The Bible—"

"Your Bible does not have an explanation for everything." Shaman spoke quietly and with respect. "Even our Legends are constantly changing and evolving as we learn more about the world around us, and as the Spirits reveal more to us."

"Speaking of Legends, didn't you have more to tell us about Stonecoats?"

Shaman poured himself another glass of whiskey.

The rest of the men did the same. Once they all drank, he closed his eyes and bowed his head.

After a few moments, his breath became haggard, and his shoulders bounced as if he was laughing.

"Are you—" Wilkerson started to ask.

Shaman opened his eyes, and his irises were gone. Huge black pupils filled the space and he spoke in an otherworldly voice:

"The Legend of the Stonecoat is one that was first told many moons ago. A beast roamed the spirit world in search of its next meal. Spirits do not offer much in the way of sustenance, so the wendigo found a path that led it to your world."

"It hunted and found wild game, but no deer, elk, bear, or buffalo was enough to satiate its need. Night after night, it killed more and more until there was no game left for man to hunt and eat."

"When man grew hungry, he started to eat his own kind."

"That is revolting!" exclaimed Corporal Miller.

"Shh, let him finish!" The lieutenant ordered.

"The wendigo saw the men fighting and eating each other. Their bellies were filled to bursting, and he cast a spell upon them to make them sleep."

"As they snored around their fires, he slit their throats one by one. The beast consumed the entire hunting party, leaving only bones and scraps of flesh by the fire."

"Its appetite finally sated, he went back to the spirit realm, where he remains to this day…until he gets hungry again."

"What a load of hogwash!" Corporal Miller stood abruptly, causing the back of his chair to hit the floor with a *thud.*

"Sit down!" The lieutenant commanded.

Begrudgingly, Miller righted his chair and sat down with a huff.

Wilkerson looked at Shaman. "Does the Legend say anything about when the Stonecoat comes back to our realm?"

Lieutenant Brant chuckled. "I thought you didn't believe this stuff."

"I don't believe the wendigo is a demon, Sir, but if it is a type of beast, then we can certainly kill it. We just need to understand its weaknesses."

"Now you're talking like a Cavalryman!" The lieutenant beamed.

"Silent Owl, tell us anything else you can about the Stonecoat."

"Legend doesn't say much else about its habits. Just that it comes back here to feed when it gets hungry. There is no mention of a season, or pattern, just that it will, and does, return to feast on those who have consumed human flesh."

David asked, "Does the Legend tell how to stop it?"

Shaman bowed his head again. After a moment, he looked back up, his pupils returning to their normal size, and his brown irises shining in the candlelight.

"No, Legend does not say. We do know it only strikes at night. And fire can weaken it. My Ancestors once fought a Stonecoat."

"How did they kill it?"

Shaman shrugged. "They didn't. The beast found one of their tribe who ate human flesh and came for him. A war party followed to bring him back, but by the time they got here, the Stonecoat was heading back into the Spirit realm."

Corporal Miller interjected. "You said they 'fought' the beast."

"They did," Shaman continued. "They used their spears and knives to drive it away. Once it crossed through the veil, the Spirits told them to stop." He shrugged. "My ancestors didn't argue with the Spirits."

"So, how do we stop it, if it is a Stonecoat we are dealing with?"

"I do not know that we can." Shaman sighed.

The lieutenant rapped on the table drawing everyone's attention away from the Native. "Men, if it can bleed, it can die. If it can die, we can kill it. For now, let us learn as much as we can about this 'beast' and its weaknesses.

"Tomorrow, we will canvas the town. I want to talk to everyone who has missing cattle, sheep that have been savaged, even if a chicken didn't lay an egg that morning, I want to know about it."

"Yes, Sir!" answered Corporal Miller.

Wilkerson asked, "Sir, what about Samson and Mr. Katzenberger?"

"What about them?"

David looked at Shaman.

The Native cleared his throat and spoke in a low voice. "There is something about that man that isn't right. He said he accidentally took us to the wrong place. That he thought the way he showed us was the residence of Mr. Katzenberger. I do not believe him."

"Then where did he take you?" asked the lieutenant.

Private Wilkerson said, "I don't know, Sir, but it certainly wasn't the home of a merchant." He blanched at the memory of what they found inside.

"After we speak with the people here, let's get some volunteers to go back there. Those people deserve a proper burial." The lieutenant met each of the men's eyes. "It is the least we can do to honor them."

"Yes, Sir," they chorused, and each lifted another glass of whiskey in a sign of respect.

# Chapter Eleven

T he next morning, the men broke into two groups. Lieutenant Brant, Corporal Miller, and Cookie went to speak with the ranchers who complained about lost or damaged livestock. Private Wilkerson and Shaman stayed in town. Their mission was to find someone who knew where Mr. Katzenberger was, or at least, the location of his residence.

After a hearty breakfast, they started at the Sheriff's office. David opened the door, while Silent Owl waited outside. The Civil War had been over for a while, but some folk still didn't take too kindly to Indians wandering about town. To limit any hesitancy on the part of the locals to offer assistance, Private Wilkerson thought it best to do as much of the talking himself as he could.

At the sound of the chime inside the door, the sheriff rose from his leather chair. "How may I help you, Son?" he asked and offered his hand.

David accepted his hand and gave him a firm, but respectful, shake. Callused fingers gripped the back of his hand; it was obvious the sheriff was used to manual labor. "Private David Wilkerson, Sheriff. We were tasked here to help you solve a bit of a mystery."

The sheriff harrumphed. "A mystery, you say? Is this about the missing cows and the sheep that got slaughtered in the middle of a field?"

"Yes, Sir, that's right. What can you tell me about that?"

"Here, let me find my notes. Just a moment." The sheriff rummaged through the stacks of paperwork on his desk, then he leaned down and opened a desk drawer. The drawer protested as if it hadn't been open in quite some time. Finally, with a squeak, the drawer came free, and the sheriff pulled a book out of it.

As the sheriff placed the book on the desk, David noticed it was bound in leather, and not much larger than a deck of playing cards. A red ribbon cut through the middle of it, marking a page.

Wilkerson asked, "Do you take all your notes in that book?"

The sheriff looked up at him and appeared startled. "Sorry, what was that?"

"Your book, Sir. Do you take all your notes in it?"

"No, Son, this book isn't my notes. This is a log of all the strange happenings in this territory since before the War. Since this County was first settled, Sheriff Moses Scott started this log to keep track of everything that couldn't simply be explained.

"We have unsolved kidnappings, murders, disappearances, and yes, even a few accounts of missing livestock. You know horse thievery is punishable by death here, don't you?"

"That is true for most of the Union, Sir."

"As it should be, Son. Here in Darke County, the same fate applies to cattle rustling. If any of these old accounts can be solved, we might have a whole lot lower population by the time your troop is through."

"That isn't exactly why we're here, Sir."

"What do you mean? Why else would you be assisting?"

David looked out the window at Shaman. He sighed. "To be honest, Sherrif, I'm not sure how much I can tell you."

"Now you wait one God darn minute! This is my County, you bet your ass you can tell me what is going on here!"

"With respect Sheriff, not until I speak with my commanding officer. In the meantime, what I can tell you is we haven't seen or heard from Mr. Katzenberger since we first arrived in town to retrieve our order."

"Did you talk to Samson?"

"Yes, and he took me and one of my associates out to his place, but to be honest, it didn't look the type of place where a business owner would reside."

"That's odd, Mr. Katzenberger has a nice spread out past Mud Creek. Where did he take you?"

"Deep in the woods to an old shack. All we found there was evidence of more missing creatures."

"What type of creatures?" The sheriff looked alarmed.

"Well, Sir, we found piles of bones, bits of flesh, and more blood than I care to remember. Have you had many people go missing lately?"

The sheriff stroked his chin and pulled at the edges of his mustache.

"Along with the reports of missing livestock, there have been a few people mentioned as disappeared, as well."

"Why didn't you mention that earlier?"

"I didn't think it relevant to the missing livestock. Besides, the people weren't from around here. They were either traveling, visiting family in the area, or passing through. It happens all the time. People come here, stay for a spell, and then go along on their merry way."

"If it is as simple as that, why would folks bother to mention if they haven't seen them around?"

"Good question."

Private Wilkerson waited for the sheriff to say more, but he didn't. After a few awkward moments, he asked, "If you aren't busy, would you mind taking me and Shaman out to Mr. Katzenberger's place?"

"Did you say 'Shaman'?"

"Yessir."

"Is that some type of injun name or something?"

"Silent Owl is one of the Shawnee and he has been helping us on our mission."

"You trust him? You know what happened back before the War."

"Yes, Sir, I know, and yes. I trust Shaman with my life."

"Alright. Go fetch your mounts and meet me here in ten minutes." The sheriff tipped his hat as Wilkerson was dismissed from his office.

The private went out the front door to where Silent Owl was waiting by a water trough. "How did that go?"

"Well enough. The Sheriff is going to take us out to Mr. Katzenberger's place. Looks like you were right about Samson. He definitely didn't take us where we thought we were going."

"Hmph," Shaman grunted. "I told you that man walks between worlds."

"And you keep telling me the 'spirits are with me.' What does any of that mean anyway?"

"In time, it will all make sense. For now, let us see about finding Mr. Katzenberger."

They saddled their mounts and met the sheriff in front of his office promptly ten minutes later. The sheriff rode a Palomino Quarter Horse with a wide blaze down his forehead. He stamped his front hooves impatiently as the sheriff conversed with one of his deputies.

The sheriff turned to Wilkerson. "That's a fine-looking boy you have there. What's his name?"

"Dawson, Sir. He's part Morgan and as surefooted as they come."

"He's a beauty, that's for sure." Pointing at his horse's ears, he said, "This is Joseph. He has been with me through thick and thin. And he has the attitude to show it."

Just then, Joseph lifted his head into the air and gave a shrill whinny, while shaking his head up and down. His white mane billowed with the effort and his forelock fell in front of his eyes.

The sheriff chuckled and reached between Joseph's ears. "Here, let me fix that for you. Can't have you unable to see when we walk down the trail."

David smiled at Shaman. It was good to see a lawman who had an affinity for his partner, especially one of the equine variety. Once everyone was settled, they moved along down a different trail through the woods.

Wilkerson pointed back behind them and said, "Samson led us down that way. Where did he take us?"

The sheriff shifted in his saddle and looked to where David indicated. "What did the structure look like again?"

"It was barely more than a one-room shack, with moss growing over the walls and on top of the roof. It looked like no one had lived there for a very long time, although the bodies were fresh enough."

"Hmm, that sounds like the old sugar shack. Years back, some pioneers made maple syrup from the local trees growing in the woods. Once the trees were tapped out, they moved on to set up shop elsewhere. It has probably been empty for a good twenty years or more."

"Would any of the locals know about that place?"

The sheriff slapped his thigh. "Boy, anyone who has lived here for any length of time at all knows about that old sugar shack! I'm honestly surprised no one has tried to stake a claim on it by now."

"Well, Sir, no one may have appealed to the land office, but someone has certainly been squatting there, at least recently."

"Good point. Let's go check on Mr. Katzenberger, then you can show me what you and Shaman found at that old shack."

"Sounds like a plan, Sheriff."

# Chapter Twelve

Lieutenant Brant, Corporal Miller, and Cookie made their way through the various shops and storefronts along the main street. At first, no one wanted to speak with them, but after the lieutenant explained what they were doing, people started to open up.

They met with a tailor who said he hadn't seen Mr. Katzenberger in nearly a week.

"Do you think something has happened to him?" he asked.

"We don't know, Sir," the lieutenant replied. "We are going to do what we can to find out."

"Do you remember what he was wearing when you last saw him?" asked Corporal Miller.

"Hmm… He dressed like normal for a day at the Mercantile. Trousers, long-sleeved shirt, pork pie hat, and boots. Come to think of it, he didn't have on a coat, which I thought was odd, considering the frigid temperature as of late. Mr. Katzenberger didn't seem concerned with the cold, just continued on his way."

"Which way was he going?"

"Away from the Store, towards Mud Creek."

"Is that the direction of his homestead?"

"Actually, yes. He lives out that way."

"Did he seem out of sorts, or in a rush?"

"He walked with a purpose, but a busy man like him always has someplace to be."

Corporal Miller offered his hand. "Thank you, Sir. We'll talk with a few more folks and see what we can deduce."

"Please do let me know once you find him."

"We will, Sir." The lieutenant promised.

Everyone else they spoke to had much the same to say. Mr. Katzenberger hadn't been seen since shortly after their troop had received their delivery. It was unlike him to leave Samson in charge for more than a few hours, and they were worried about him.

"Maybe we should try the telegraph office." Cookie suggested. "He may have sent word to a relation about his plans."

Lieutenant Brant clapped Cookie on his stout back. "Excellent thinking!"

They approached the telegraph office about fifteen minutes later. It was located clear on the other side of the town, near the Greenville Fire Department.

The office had a false-front roofline, with thick wooden pillars on the front corners of the building. The glass windows were yellowed with age, and a small shingle hung from the porch that read, "Telegraph Office."

As they entered, a bell announced their arrival and the operator rose from behind his desk. "How may I help you, gentlemen?"

"We are looking for Mr. Katzenberger and need to know if he sent or received any messages in the last week."

"Let me check my records. Is he in some kind of trouble? It's not every day the Cavalry comes looking for one of our entrepreneurs."

"No, we just understand he has not been seen in nearly a week and are trying to ascertain his whereabouts."

The operator nodded. "The last message received was the confirmation of a large order of military supplies." He looked up at them. "I'm assuming that order was placed for your troop." The lieutenant confirmed. "I see. He has not sent any messages within that time period."

Cookie asked, "What about before then?"

"It isn't customary for me to divulge the contents of people's private correspondence."

Cookie held his hands up in a placating gesture. "Of course not, but any information you can give us will help to find him."

"Is he missing?" The operator's voice went hoarse with concern.

"That is what we are trying to find out. As we said earlier, no one has seen him in nearly a week and people are worried about him."

"He did receive a message from his sister about a month back. Let me go into the back. Just a moment."

Corporal Miller gave the lieutenant a questioning look.

"He has no reason not to help us." The lieutenant assured him.

After a few moments, the Operator came back with a piece of paper in his hand. "Here is the message."

Lieutenant Brant read through it. "She wished him a Happy New Year and wanted to verify he received the gift she sent him for the Christmas holiday. Nothing of consequence."

"Did he send a reply?" Cookie peeked over the lieutenant's shoulder to read the note.

The Operator placed his index finger on his chin. "Come to think of it, no, he didn't."

"Is that usual?" Corporal Miller crossed his arms over his chest.

"Most folks reply back to their loved ones, but I don't know Mr. Katzenberger well enough to answer that question."

"Very well," said the lieutenant. "Thank you for your time."

They exited the office and walked back down the muddy street. Their boots squelched in the deeper puddles and drops of muck gathered around their ankles.

Corporal Miller asked, "Now what, Sir?"

"Now, we wait to see what Private Wilkerson and Shaman find."

Joseph and Dawson trotted down the path toward Mr. Katzenberger's residence. Private Wilkerson marveled at how beautiful the trees looked out here. Unlike the forest where they had camped, these trees looked healthy and strong. The understory was thinned, and the canopy teemed with birds chirping merrily in the afternoon sun.

As they rounded a bend in the trail, a large home came into sight. Unlike most of the homes in this region, Mr. Katzenberger's residence was painted white with tiles on the roof. It had a wrap-around porch and more windows than David could count at first glance.

In the driveway sat a covered wagon, but no horses were hitched to it. Other than the birds, there were no noticeable signs of life.

David turned to the sheriff. "Does anyone else live here?"

The sheriff shook his head. "Mr. Katzenberger's wife passed away a few years ago. The mercantile is his legacy and he does his best to help all of the townsfolk as best he can."

"What happens to the store when he passes?" asked Wilkerson.

The sheriff bristled. "Son, that is between Mr. Wilkerson and his attorney."

Private Wilkerson blushed in embarrassment. "I meant no disrespect."

The sheriff nodded and walked Joseph out to a hitching post near the house's front door. He dismounted and tied the leather reins long enough for his mount to nibble at some grass poking its way through the frozen ground.

He reached for the .44 caliber Smith & Wesson Model 3 in his hip holster as he approached the door. "Mr. Katzenberger! Are you home?"

Silence was his answer.

Private Wilkerson shouldered his rifle from Dawson's back to cover the sheriff, just in case.

Silent Owl slid down his war pony's withers and stalked silently to the opposite side of the door from the sheriff.

The sheriff nodded at him and called for Mr. Katzenberger once more, followed by a loud *knock, knock, knock*. There was no answer.

Private Wilkerson clucked his tongue to get the sheriff's attention. He made a motion with his arm to indicate he was taking his horse around the back of the house.

The sheriff nodded and holstered his top-break revolver. He motioned to Shaman to walk around the back of the house as he turned to walk to the opposite side of the residence.

As he neared the back corner of the house, his stomach clenched. He placed his left elbow in front of his face to block the stench of rotting flesh assaulting his nose. Pulling his revolver from the holster on his right hip, he slowly peered around the corner.

The sheriff saw Private Wilkerson hunched over the side of Dawson dry heaving. Looking along the back porch, Silent Owl approached the young soldier.

Sheriff Nelson continued the length of the porch to a pile of bones and flesh. A dried gout of blood smeared across the wall behind the corpse. His boots stuck to the floorboards as he got closer to the body.

An exposed ribcage shined blindingly despite the shadows cast by the roofline. It appeared all the internal organs had been removed. Strips of flesh clung to the bones, but no muscle could be seen.

The sheriff swallowed hard and walked over to Private Wilkerson. Shaman had his hand on the young man's shoulder, and he was speaking in low soothing tones.

Wilkerson was pale, his eyes bloodshot and wet with tears.

"Are you alright, son?" the sheriff asked.

David stood to look the sheriff in the eye. "No, Sir. I am not 'alright.' People in your town are being massacred and forgotten. Tomorrow, my troop is going back to the shack where we found more corpses so *we* can give them a proper burial. My question is why? And what are you doing about it, *Sheriff*?"

The sheriff stiffened. "I'll forgive your outburst on account of shock, but you best watch your tone, *boy!* I didn't know anything about these corpses until *your troop* rolled into my town. How do I know you or one of yours isn't responsible?"

Wilkerson slipped out of the saddle and took a step closer to the sheriff.

Shaman gripped his shoulder before he could do anything stupid. "We should go. Our job here is done."

"What do you mean done?" asked David.

"We found Mr. Katzenberger." He pointed at the corpse on the back deck. "Now, we need to inform your commanding officer and await further orders."

Wilkerson glared at the sheriff but turned and walked back to Dawson. He thrust his foot in the stirrup and mounted quickly. "Shaman is right. "I need to report to my lieutenant."

The sheriff relaxed his fists and slowly rolled his head across his shoulders. He met David's eyes and said, "That is a fine idea. When you're done, bring your men back to my office." He looked at the remains on the porch and hung his head. "I'll help you bury them."

"Sir, we found Mr. Katzenberger." Private Wilkerson had a half-empty glass of whiskey in one hand and a mug of beer in the other. He sagged in his seat, the weight of the world firmly planted on his wiry shoulders.

Lieutenant Brant took the whiskey glass out of his hand and drained it. "It looks to me like you've had enough of that."

David nodded and placed his hands on his knees. "I just don't understand it, Sir. Mr. Katzenberger seemed a nice man. Why would the Stonecoat go after him?"

Lieutenant Brant looked at Shaman. "That is a fine question. Any ideas?"

Silent Owl spoke solemnly. "Legend tells of the wendigo attacking men who consume human flesh. Perhaps, Mr.

Katzenberger wasn't a 'nice man' after all. Or the corpse we found was someone else entirely." He shrugged.

The lieutenant sighed. "Our problem is that we don't know enough about the people in this town to come to any conclusions. What we do know is there is some type of creature, we believe it is a Stonecoat, or a wendigo, attacking people and mutilating them.

"We also know people aren't the only victims. Livestock is missing as well. So, what are we to do?"

Shaman leaned forward. "We track it."

"Track what?" asked Wilkerson.

"We need to determine who, or what, was the last victim. Find a blood trail and follow it. Determine if it really is a Stonecoat or if something, or someone else is responsible."

The lieutenant nodded. "I don't have any better ideas."

Private Wilkerson sat forward in his seat. "I almost forgot, Sir. The Sheriff asked us all to meet him at his office. He wants to help us with the bodies."

The troop made their way to the sheriff's office shortly thereafter. Shaman helped Private Wilkerson stagger through the door and directed him to a high-backed chair in the entryway.

As soon as David's hind end touched the seat, the sheriff burst into the room.

"Well, well, well."

"What is that supposed to mean?" asked Lieutenant Brant.

"As I told your *Private*, people in my town haven't gone missing until after you all showed up here. I should arrest your troop and place you all in confinement."

Cookie made a move towards the sheriff, but the lieutenant placed his hand on his shoulder.

"Sheriff, I understand your concern, but the bodies my private found have been there for a long while, much longer than a week."

"How can you be so sure?"

"Due to the status of the bodies. Come with us, and we'll show you."

The sheriff looked out the window. "Night will fall soon. It's better to go out there in the daylight. Besides," he looked at Private Wilkerson, "we probably want to have all our wits about us."

The lieutenant looked at David, then nodded at the Sheriff.

"Agreed. We'll meet you back here at first light."

Corporal Miller eased Wilkerson up the stairs and into his bed. As soon as his head hit the pillow, he was sawing logs like a lumberjack.

Miller headed down to the bar and stopped at the head of the stairs. From below him, female voices chorused throughout the room. He had to listen closely to make out the words. *Our Father, who art in Heaven…* They were reciting the Lord's Prayer.

He bounded down the stairs and was stopped by Lieutenant Brant.

"I'll handle them," he said as he walked over to the older lady from the other night. She was on her knees in the middle of the floor with the other ladies from before. They all had their hands folded in prayer and their eyes squeezed shut. He leaned down and asked, "Miss Prudence, was it?"

She continued reciting her prayer in unison with her fellows and ignored him.

"Ma'am?" The lieutenant persisted.

Corporal Miller walked up to his blond friend from the night before. "Hello again. Did you miss me?"

She glanced up at him and smiled wryly, then looked over at Prudence.

Prudence shook her head and continued to pray.

When their prayer was finished, the lieutenant spoke. "Ladies, what is this all about?"

Miller's friend opened her mouth to answer, but Prudence shushed her.

"Sir," she began, "this is about bringing our menfolk back to the Lord. Liquor is clouding your minds. You need to see the error of your ways and repent!"

"Ma'am, I assure you I have done plenty wrong, but none of those acts were performed while I was in the drink." The lieutenant chuckled.

"Laugh all you want. Our crusade is just beginning. We're not done, yet." With that, she stood and rallied the other women around her. "Come, ladies. Perhaps, the saloon will be more receptive to our message."

Corporal Miller reached out for his blond friend, but she pulled away. "Not tonight, darling. Maybe tomorrow," she whispered as she blew him a kiss.

Prudence turned beet red and stormed out the door, her skirts swishing behind her.

Miller placed his hands over his heart and smiled as he watched the ladies leave.

Lieutenant Brant rapped him on the head. "Remember why we were originally called here. Those ladies might be up to some trouble."

"Oh, they're trouble all right…my favorite kind."

The troop rode to the sheriff's office the next morning in silence. Dawn had just broken over the horizon and the empty street was filled with warm sunlight.

Private Wilkerson leaned back in his saddle lifting his face to the warmth. "Today will be a good day."

"What makes you say that?" asked Corporal Miller.

"I can just feel it."

Silent Owl looked at Private Wilkeson and gave him a small smile. "The Spirits are with you."

The lieutenant strode to the front door and tried the knob. It was locked. He bent down to peer into the darkened office. Looking behind him at his men, he announced, "No one is here."

Cookie scoffed. "Maybe it's too early for him."

Lieutenant Brant glowered. "I doubt that. Corporal, check the back. The rest of you, fan out!"

The men obeyed the lieutenant's commands without hesitation. Private Wilkerson and Shaman went to the right, Cookie went left, and Corporal Miller disappeared around the back side of the building.

Cookie reached for his Colt Dragoon in a shoulder holster and waited. He didn't hear a sound, not even the horses breathing behind him. Something hit him, hard, on the back of his head and his vision swam. He grabbed for his weapon as he fell forward, but his weight pinned his arm beneath his bulk.

He shouted as he rolled over to his back. Looking down on him was the most fearsome sight he had ever beheld. A long fang-filled snout sat inches away from his own nose. He could smell its rank breath and see bits of flesh from its last meal stuck in its teeth.

The eyes were wide in the morning light and round like a human's. Protruding from its head were a pair of long antlers, reminiscent of an Eastern Elk.

Cookie's breath caught in his chest. He laid there staring fate in the face for what felt like an eternity. From his left, he heard bootsteps hitting the frozen ground. Shouts and yells preceded the arrival of his men.

The beast huffed in his face once more, drool dripping onto Cookie's beard, before it loped off and out of sight.

Cookie gagged. *Crack!* He bolted to his feet in time to see the sheriff pointing his long gun in the direction the beast had fled.

Staring at him, Cookie shouted, "Do you still want to place us in confinement?"

The Sheriff lowered his weapon as his arms started to shake. He looked from Cookie to the rest of the men as they gathered around him.

"What in Hell was that thing? And why is it here in your town?" Cookie stalked towards the sheriff.

"If I didn't see that with my own eyes, I'd never believe it. Ya'll better come inside. I'll put on a pot of coffee."

"Coffee? That thing just tried to eat my face and you're offering me *coffee*!" Cookie was fit to be tied.

"Sergeant." Lieutenant Brant squinted at Cookie. "Let's see what the sheriff has to share with us."

Cookie mumbled under his breath as he kicked at the loose dirt with his boot.

Corporal Miller sidled over to Wilkerson. "A good day, huh?"

David grinned sheepishly at the corporal. "Cookie didn't get eaten. That counts as a good day, right?"

Silent Owl walked over to Cookie and raised his tomahawk.

"What are you doing?" Wilkerson shrieked and ran between the two men.

Shaman lowered his tomahawk and ran his left hand through Cookie's beard. He wiped his hand on the blade of the tomahawk and sheathed it behind his back. "According to Legend, stonecoat saliva can strengthen metal and make blades more sharp." He spun on his heel and walked towards the Sheriff's office.

Wilkerson looked from Silent Owl's receding form to Cookie and shook his head.

Cookie clapped him on the shoulder and pulled him towards the promise of coffee.

"Why don't we start at the beginning?" the sheriff suggested. "You men came to me asking about missing folks. I didn't think much of it until I went out with your private there and saw Mr. Katzenberg lying dead on his back porch.

"My blood was up after that, and I may have said a few words that I now regret." He looked expectantly at Private Wilkerson.

David said, "I too may have not been in the best mindset after what we saw together. I apologize for any disrespect."

"Apology accepted. Now," he continued as he pulled out his notebook, "this is a list of people whose whereabouts are unknown." He held up the page to show more than twenty names.

"You said people didn't start disappearing until we got here!" Wilkerson cried incredulously.

The Sheriff bristled and said, "I apologized, remember?"

David stared him down but said nothing.

"As I was saying, most of these people were not from here. Mostly merchants or people traveling through to see relations or moving west to find their fortunes."

"And you are sharing this with us now, why?" asked Lieutenant Brant.

"Because, if we can match up those bodies you found with the names on this list, we can offer their families some solace. Besides," he looked again at Wilkerson, "it don't feel right burying someone without their name on a headstone."

David nodded at the Sheriff and allowed a small smile to cross his face.

"Now then, let's head out to that shack you were telling me about. I'll have the coroner follow us in his ambulance so we can bring everyone back to the undertaker."

The lieutenant stood and addressed his men, "You heard the sheriff. Everyone mount up and move out!"

They mounted their horses and Private Wilkerson led the troop down the trail they had followed with Samson.

Despite the morning light, shadows danced across the trail causing the horses to snort nervously and dance along the frozen ground. The men patted their mounts' withers to calm them and spoke in soothing tones while keeping their heads up and scanning for any signs of a threat.

Through the darkness, Wilkerson spied the shack in the distance, an unearthly green light emanating from one of its broken windows. He held up his fist to call a halt.

The lieutenant rode up next to him and asked, "Was that here before?"

"No," David whispered. "When we were here before, everything was dark. The only light came from outside when we opened the front door."

Lieutenant Brant rode over to Silent Owl who had slipped off his pony's back and waited in the rear of their small formation. "What do you think?"

"I think the Stonecoat is here."

"In the daylight? I thought they only attacked at night."

"I spoke with Sergeant Taylor, and he swears he has never consumed human flesh. I thought the Stonecoat only attacked cannibals." He shrugged. "Perhaps, we are not dealing with a wendigo."

Wilkerson overheard their exchange and shuddered. "So, what do we do?"

Shaman spoke. "We do not have enough men to vanquish the beast. Even my people struggled with a full war party of fifty men. I say we wait for it to leave, then you can recover the bodies and bury your dead."

"Wait for it to leave?" Cookie stammered. "Why are we standing around waiting for that thing to attack us? I say we hightail it back to town and come back later." He looked at Silent Owl. "If fifty injun warriors weren't enough to kill a Stonecoat, what chance do we have?"

Shaman met the lieutenant's gaze. "What say you?"

"You know the Legend of the Stonecoat better than the rest of us. If you think we should wait, then I agree. We will wait." Lieutenant Brant stared at the sugar shack.

Corporal Miller dismounted. "I think that is horseshit! How many more people have to die before we can stop it? It might not even be this beast you call a Stonecoat. I say we charge in there and send it straight back to Hell where it came from!"

The Lieutenant cleared his throat. "Corporal, I appreciate your passion for the mission; however, Silent Owl is right. I won't have us risking our lives haphazardly. We need to know what, exactly, we are dealing with."

"Wilkerson, take Shaman with you and see what you can find. The rest of us will hold here and wait for your return."

David gulped audibly and his skin paled at the thought of facing down a wendigo. "Sir," his teeth chattered, "are you certain this is our best course of action?"

"Are you questioning orders?"

Wilkerson slowly shook his head.

The sheriff dismounted Joseph and walked over to David. "If it makes you feel any better, I'll cover you. At the first sign of trouble, I've got my rifle to back you up."

Wilkerson gulped again, then nodded.

"Now that's settled," said the Lieutenant. "Carry on."

David and Shaman crept silently toward the shack, hunched over with their weapons ready. The stench of death and rotted flesh greeted them the closer they got to the structure.

Taking a deep breath to help settle his raging stomach, Wilkerson approached one of the shattered windows and ducked down underneath the sill.

The sheriff kept his distance, rifle at the ready, and watched for any sign of the strange beast that attacked Cookie earlier that day.

Silent Owl sat under another broken window on the same side of the house as David glanced inside. He ducked back down quickly and muttered an Algonquin curse.

"What did you see?" asked Wilkerson.

"More bodies."

"How many more?"

Shaman shook his head. "Too many."

"Is the beast here?"

"If so, I do not see it."

"I'm going to take a closer look." Private Wilkerson duck-walked to the door and found it open, just as they had left it. He peered inside through the crack between the doorjamb and the door itself. Green light flowed towards him, and he heard the steady beat of drums. Along with the steady thrum, was a shrill whistling sound. It set him on edge and caused the hairs on the back of his neck to stand and salute.

Wilkerson took a deep breath and listened closer. The whistling resolved into a tune he had heard somewhere before. From behind him, the men shouted. He jumped backward away from the door to see the commotion.

Cookie staggered towards him awkwardly. He wore a blank expression on his face, and his eyes glowed a pale yellow, just like the eyes David had seen somewhere before.

The private realized those were the same eyes that stared at him from within a fire their first night in these cursed woods. Wilkerson put his hands out to stop Cookie, but the Sergeant dropped his shoulder and sent him flying into the side of the shack. The rickety building let out a loud creak as timbers snapped and groaned all around him.

Wilkerson stood quickly and grabbed Cookie around the waist at a headlong sprint. The two men tumbled away from the sugar shack just in time. The roof collapsed onto the structure sending splinters and shattered bones in all directions.

"Wha – what happened?" asked a dazed Cookie.

David gasped for air, then said, "I was hoping you could tell me."

Cookie stood and offered a hand to the private. He hoisted him to his feet and shook his head as if to clear it.

"I – I thought I saw Red standing there. He was waving at me and beckoned me inside. It looked like he was in trouble. All I could think was to help him, so I headed to the door. You got in my way, so I pushed you." He looked down at the private. "Sorry about that," he said sheepishly.

"It's alright, Cookie. I'm just glad you're ok."

The sheriff and the lieutenant came over to check on the men.

"Wait, where is Shaman?" asked Wilkerson.

The pile of rubble shifted as a dark-skinned arm eased its way out from underneath. Corporal Miller ran over and gripped it. He pushed pieces of the roof away from the arm.

"I need some help here!" he yelled.

The rest of the troop gathered around and started throwing timber, roofing material, and debris away from the failed structure.

After a good long while, they uncovered Silent Owl and pulled him free of the debris. He stood slowly and looked at the pile that attempted to give him an early grave. Smiling at Private Wilkerson, he said, "I guess the Spirits are with me today, too."

David grabbed him about the shoulders and pulled him into a fierce hug. "I'm relieved you are alright. How did you get inside without us noticing?"

"Everyone was watching Cookie, so I snuck in through the window while you were distracted. Other than that strange light, there was nothing inside. I heard the frame creaking and tried to get out, but the building collapsed before I could." He looked at the corporal. "Thank you for saving me."

Corporal Miller's face reddened. "Aw, heck!" He waved away the gratitude. "All I did was move some firewood around."

The lieutenant interjected, "That isn't exactly true. You saw his hand and rendered aid without an order. Then you rallied the rest of us to help dig him out. I say that deserves a commendation."

"Sir, I—" For once, the corporal was speechless.

The sheriff cleared his throat. "As much as I hate to disrupt this tender moment, we still have a pile of bodies inside to identify."

"With the building collapsed, how do you intend to do that?" asked the lieutenant.

The coroner came over. During all the previous excitement, he had sheltered in the safety of his ambulance. "We start at the top," he suggested. "Pull as much of the building material away as we can and put it in one pile. Next, we find the bodies. If at all possible, we separate the bodies and load them into the ambulance.

"Once we get them back to the undertaker, we will do what we can to identify them."

The men were not excited about this task, but they all realized it needed to be done. Cookie broke the uncomfortable silence. "Once we finish up, I'll pay for the first round of drinks at the saloon!"

That earned him a whoop from the corporal and a "Here, here" from everyone else. With the promise of a liquid reward at the end of an awful day, the men set to work.

# Chapter Thirteen

The men's breath created a fog that formed around the collapsed shack. Despite the sunlight in the clearing, they found it hard to see through the mist. More times than not, Corporal Miller reached into the pile for a piece of timber only to accidentally smack Cookie on his bald pate.

"Would you watch what you're doing?" The sergeant growled.

"I said I was sorry." Corporal Miller turned back towards the pile more carefully this time.

On the other side of the shack, Private Wilkerson and Shaman had managed to pull away most of the building material and cleared out the area with a huge pile of bones and bodies. With the coroner's assistance, they did their best to keep the remains of each individual separate from the rest of the corpses.

After a few hours of grueling work, and not so few muttered curses, Lieutenant Brant called for a break. "We're making good progress and I think the coroner has enough loaded up to take back to the undertaker.

"Wilkerson, I want you and Silent Owl to scout around the building. See if you can find any evidence of who, or what, was using this structure."

"Yes, Sir," David replied.

The sheriff stepped over to the lieutenant. "You have a good group of men here. Considering the task at hand, they all acted professionally and hardly complained."

"We are Cavalrymen. There is a certain code of honor we subscribe to. It helps when things get difficult, or in this case, unexpected."

The sheriff surveyed the clearing and watched the men as they rested. "I can see that. Do you ever have the need for civilians to assist you?"

Lieutenant Brant chuckled. "Sheriff, I would hardly consider you a civilian."

"True, but things have been much more interesting since you guys showed up in my county."

"Are you saying you need more adventure in your life?" The lieutenant quirked an eyebrow.

The sheriff sighed. "Not exactly…"

"Good, because I recommend you be careful what you ask for."

"Sir!" Wilkerson shouted from the backside of what used to be the shack.

"What do you have, Private?"

Cookie and the corporal stood from where they were seated on a rotted log and jogged over to join the lieutenant and David.

"It's footprints, Sir."

"Like the ones we saw our first night in these cursed woods?" asked Cookie.

The lieutenant looked pointedly from Cookie to the private.

"Yes, Sergeant. The very same."

Lieutenant Brant shook his head. "Very well. Breaktime is over. Let's pull out as many more as we can before the coroner returns. Then, I believe Cookie promised us refreshments."

"Aye," said Cookie with a gleam in his eye. "That I did!"

They continued recovering bones from the shack for another couple of hours. Instead of everyone working on the pile at once, the lieutenant ordered them to work in shifts with a sentry posted in case the beast returned.

As soon as the coroner's wagon approached, Wilkerson and Shaman brought out the last body. Bones seemed to glow in the fading light and as the sun set, mist formed throughout the clearing. In the distance, the men heard a whistle.

"Alright, men! That's our cue. Let's return to town." Lieutenant Brant looked at the sheriff.

He nodded and said, "Tomorrow, I will work with the coroner to match up the remains with the list of missing persons. Once we're done, any that haven't been identified will be buried. I already spoke with the local pastor and there is a section of the graveyard reserved for them to be laid to rest."

The lieutenant removed his hat and covered his heart with it. Bowing his head, he said, "We will be there to assist."

"Thank you," said the sheriff. "Now, did I hear something about your sergeant buying everyone whiskey?"

Lieutenant Brant laughed and clapped the sheriff on the shoulder. "That you did, that you did."

As the mounted men emerged from the woods, the ambulance followed behind. Its wooden wheels creaked and groaned under the weight of so many bodies. The draft horses pulling it huffed with exertion and snorted in complaint.

Their unease caused the Cavalry mounts to tense and Dawson sidestepped down the trail. Wilkerson reached his right hand down to his withers and gave him a gentle pat. "Easy boy, the hard part is done. We're heading back to the stable now. You're alright…" he said in a soothing tone. Despite the calmness of his words, he couldn't help but feel they were being watched. The hairs on the back of his neck stood up, and gooseflesh bloomed under his shirtsleeves.

The wind howled around them even though there had been nary a breeze the rest of the day. On the wind, a sound was carried forward: a haunting whistle that made David's heart race inside his chest. "Did you hear that?" he yelled as his voice cracked.

Cookie responded, "Yep," and rode closer to Wilkerson to help him calm Dawson. It was to no avail.

Dawson reared up, his forelegs thrashing into the air, and he whinnied high and shrill.

David leaned forward in his saddle to keep his center of gravity over his mount's, but as Dawson's legs thrashed down to the ground, he stumbled, sending the private over his head and onto the frozen mud.

Cookie grabbed for Dawson's reins and galloped his Clydesdale after to keep from being pulled out of his own saddle.

The whistling got closer. Wilkerson was on his back gasping for air, but there was none to be found. The only wind available had been knocked out of him, and the other was none too friendly. When he was finally able to draw a ragged breath, he opened his eyes to find the rest of the men gone.

He was alone on the trail, looking up at a pitch-black sky. *It can't be dark already. We were just heading back to town at dusk.*

The view of the sky was blotted out by a face leaning over him. Yellow eyes gleamed like a mountain lion's and hot breath washed over his nose, causing him to gag. He swallowed and sat up slowly.

"You again?"

"Hello, David. I told you to join us. Now you don't have a choice." Red reached down and pulled Wilkerson to his feet.

He staggered and sagged against Red despite wanting to get away.

"I already told you, 'no.'" Wilkerson pushed away from Red, sending himself backward and landing on his hind end. "In fact, I have a better idea." He looked up at Red from his embarrassing vantage point. With flushed cheeks, he said, "Why don't you come with me? We can talk to the lieutenant and let him know you're alive. He'll be so relieved."

"Don't be naïve. What can the lieutenant possibly do for me that my new master can't? He brought my mare back from the dead. He has so much power and he will share it with me...and with you!"

"You're a fool," snarled David. "Your *master* is the one who annihilated your mare in the first place. If it wasn't for him, we would be riding back home getting ready for some rest and recuperation. Now, we have to bury the bodies of strangers and stop him, it, before he kills anyone else."

"You don't understand. My master only kills those who deserve it."

"Then why did it go after Cookie? Cookie never ate anyone!"

Red jumped back from David. "You lie!"

Wilkerson pushed himself to his feet. "No, I have never lied to you, and I never will! You are, were, my best friend. Come back with me and let me help you!"

"I-I can't. It's too late. I already made a promise."

"Then squelch on your promise. Take it back."

"It's not that simple."

Red started to say more, but someone grabbed David's belt loops and pulled him away. "Wait! Red!"

Cold water sloshed over his face, and he gasped at the sensation. "What happened?"

"When you tumbled off your horse, you landed on your back and hit your head on a rock. You were out cold. We had to throw you in the ambulance to get you back to town." Corporal Miller's eyes were filled with concern.

"Town?" David looked around. They were back inside the Wagner House, and he was lying in a bed on the second floor. Night hadn't fallen yet, and lazy light peered in through the curtains.

He rubbed the back of his head and his hand came away with blood. Wilkerson winced and took a deep breath.

"You were lucky," said the lieutenant. "Cookie was able to get your horse safely into the livery."

"I should go check on him. Is Dawson alright?"

The lieutenant pushed David's shoulders gently back to the bed. "Your horse is fine; it's you I'm worried about."

"I'm fine," Wilkerson protested.

"Then why were you talking to Red?" asked Shaman.

"I wasn't talking to anyone! You said yourself, I was out cold."

Silent Owl shook his head. "Do you often speak when you are dreaming?"

"Not that I know of. Why?"

"Well, you talk a lot when you are having a vision."

"A vision?"

"Yes, what else would you call a conversation with a friend who is missing."

David sighed. "I think Red is in trouble."

"Of course he is," said the lieutenant. "He ran off while his troop was on a mission."

"That isn't what I mean, Sir. He kept talking about his 'master.'"

"Master? You think the Stonecoat has conscripted him?"

"I don't know, Sir." Wilkerson turned to Shaman. "Do you have any ideas?"

"The wendigo can hunt alone or in packs. I have heard they are capable of turning humans into one of them, but I do not know how or why it is done."

Wilkerson hung his head. "Sir, what are we going to do?"

"Right now, we can't worry about Red. Tomorrow, we have people to lay to rest. After that, we need to find this beast and stop it."

"Sir, what if Red gets in the way?"

"Let's hope it doesn't come to that."

# Chapter Fourteen

Silence greeted the men as they entered the saloon. Instead of a lively environment, the patrons were solemn, staring into their drinks as if searching for the meaning of life.

Sergeant Taylor swaggered to the bar to open a tab.

"Better drink your fill tonight," advised the barkeep.

"Why's that?" asked Cookie.

The barkeep pointed to a table in the corner where five ladies sat, hands clasped in prayer, eyes closed, and lips moving silently.

Lieutenant Brant followed his gaze and noticed Prudence among the ladies. He sighed. "I see they haven't given up on their crusade."

"No, Sir," said the barkeep as he wiped down glasses and filled them with whiskey. "Tonight is our last night in service. These ladies are bad for business, and I won't be placing another order until they get bored and find another cause."

Sheriff Nelson bellied up to the bar and pulled out a stool. "In that case, we make good on the Sergeant's offer. I'll let him get the first round. I will cover the second."

"Your money is no good here," said the barkeep. "I've a feeling you'll be earning your salary sooner rather than later."

Cookie signed a strip of paper and placed a few notes next to it. "I think we'll all be earning our pay before we know it."

The Lieutenant nodded and raised his glass.

Private Wilkerson downed his libation and made his way over to the ladies' table. "Miss Prudence, may I sit a spell?"

She finished her silent prayer and looked up at him with big brown eyes. "What can I do for you? Are you here to chase us out, or would you like to join us in prayer?"

David pulled out the chair next to her and waited for her to nod before he sat. "I am curious about your crusade. Why is it so important to you that the men in this town stop drinking libations?"

She thought for a moment and started to shake, her brown curls falling into her face. When she looked at him again, her eyes were wet and bloodshot.

"I'm sorry, Ma'am, I didn't mean to upset you."

"It's not you." She sniffed and rubbed her nose with a handkerchief. "When I was young, my pa was a mean bastard." She made to spit on the floor but thought better of it. "Forgive me Lord for my curse," she whispered. "After a hard day in the fields, he would come inside for supper and drink. By the time his plate was empty, his glass would be as well. Ma would fill him another glass." She closed her eyes and took a deep breath. "By the time he had three or four refills, he would start hollerin'." Her face took on a faraway look as she relived the memory. "My brothers would get the belt, and I—" Prudence couldn't meet Wilkerson's eyes. "I was made to do things no daughter should do for her pa." She started sobbing again.

The private reached for her hand and she moved it away. "I apologize. Just wanted to offer you some comfort."

"Please don't touch me," she whispered.

Wilkerson pulled his hand back and set it in his lap. "You know not all men get mean when they have whiskey." He motioned around the room. "Most of us get loud and tell a few tall tales, but we would never force ourselves on a woman."

"Be that as it may, you and your soldiers are not every man. Most of the men I see turn into a completely different creature when they reach the bottom of their glass. It's best to prevent the beasts from entering society. That is why my sisters and I are here. And we will remain here, and at every establishment serving libations until no more drops of whiskey touch a man's lips."

She raised her face defiantly to the private.

"Thank you," he said as he stood. Pushing his chair in he added, "I can't promise that these men won't turn into beasts with or without whiskey."

Prudence glared at him as he took his leave.

Private Wilkerson walked over to the bar to join the others. Cookie handed him a glass as he sat.

"What was that all about?" asked Lieutenant Brant.

Wilkerson sipped his whiskey, the amber fluid lighting a fire as it ran down his throat. "I was curious why Miss Prudence wanted this crusade. Turns out her pa was a mean drunk and abused her and her brothers." He took another sip. "She believes if men stop imbibing, they will become more pure than the driven snow."

Corporal Miller laughed. "Don't she know men ain't pure?"

"That's what I tried to tell her, but she is convinced. Men will be beasts drunk or sober."

"Let's hope we don't encounter too many of them while we are here." Lieutenant Brant poured himself another glass. "Besides, we have an early day tomorrow." He looked at the sheriff.

Sheriff Nelson tipped his hat. "I'll see you in the morning."

Dawn light filtered through the window and landed softly on Private Wilkerson's face. He snorted and rolled away from the light, clinging to the last few moments of peace before the day began.

A knock on his door brought him to his feet.

"Good morning, David," Silent Owl greeted.

"Shaman." David turned from the door and gathered his things to get ready.

"I will see you downstairs." Silent Owl nodded at the Private.

David dressed quickly and rubbed his bloodshot eyes. He gripped the disc of obsidian hanging around his neck and said a silent prayer. With his mind prepared for today's tasks, he joined his troop at their usual table for breakfast.

"Morning Wilkerson!" Corporal Miller handed him a mug of coffee.

"Private," greeted the lieutenant as David helped himself to a slab of ham.

"Morning, Sir," David replied after swallowing a morsel of the salty meat.

Cookie joined them a moment later and loaded his plate to the point of food sliding off and into his lap. He yanked a strip of bacon from his trousers and tore a piece off with his teeth. "I could get used to grub like this every day."

"Don't get too comfortable," Lieutenant Brant said. "Once we complete this mission, we'll be off to who knows where."

"Speaking of that, Sir," David looked at the Lieutenant, "what exactly is our plan?"

"After we lay the dead to rest, we need to vanquish the beast that attacked them. I received word that more cattle were slaughtered last night. It seems the more this Stonecoat kills, the more it goes after."

Silent Owl spoke. "That is in line with Legend. The beast's hunger can never be sated. It will keep killing, keep eating, until there is nothing left for it to hunt."

"Unless we stop it, right?" asked Wilkerson.

Shaman nodded. "Stonecoats get their name from their sturdy hide. Knives and tomahawks do not inflict mortal damage. Even your firesticks cannot harm one."

"Then how are we going to stop it?" asked Corporal Miller.

Lieutenant Brant looked at Silent Owl.

"The Stonecoat come out at night and shy away from light. No one has ever seen one near a fire."

"But, it came to me in a dream through the campfire." Wilkerson protested.

"Yes, you were in a vision state. The rules of the dream world are not the same as here."

"Also, he was wearing a cloak…" David added.

"A cloak is going to protect this thing from fire?" Corporal Miller slapped his knee. "This is beyond ridiculous!"

Lieutenant Brant tapped him on the shoulder. "Corporal, I have seen many things I can't explain. Trust Silent Owl and we will all make it through this."

"How can you be so sure?" asked Cookie.

Wilkerson looked the Lieutenant in the eye. "He has faith."

The men finished the rest of their meal in silence. They made their way to the law office where Sheriff Nelson was waiting for them.

He extended his hand to Cookie. "Thank you again for the fine libations last night Sergeant."

"'Twasn't nothing. Thank you for arranging the burial for the people we found in the old sugar shack."

"Speaking of, let me escort you to the undertaker. The coroner is there with his ambulance ready to take everyone to the graveyard."

The men removed their hats and followed the Sheriff to the far side of town.

# Chapter Fifteen

The undertaker's office was as glum and mournsome as the men's hearts. Lieutenant Brant offered his hand as he looked around the room. "Where are all the caskets?" he asked.

"We didn't have enough material for that many, but we have five ready to go into the ground." The undertaker looked at his boots. "We'll be busy fashioning the rest of them as quickly as we can, but with as many as you found, it'll take us the better part of a week to finish."

The lieutenant nodded. "We appreciate your efforts, as I'm sure do their families."

"Thank you, Sir." The undertaker led the men to the back where five simple caskets sat in a row. The men positioned themselves around the first and lifted it gently. They walked slowly and carefully under the weight and placed it into the waiting ambulance.

The driver slid the first casket all the way to the front of the wagon and reached out for the next. They repeated this process until all five caskets were loaded.

Cookie addressed the undertaker. "I'll ride with you if that's alright?" At the undertaker's nod, he climbed up onto the buckboard. The draft horses tossed their heads and stamped their hooves, anxious to get moving.

"Easy there fellas; we're not going too far." The undertaker lifted the reins and steered the horses to the cemetery.

White pillars greeted the ambulance as it made its way to the empty plot. The wagon trundled slowly along the path and stopped next to a large patch of earth with five freshly dug graves. "They worked all night to be ready for us." The undertaker stopped the wagon and motioned for Cookie to join him in the back.

Cookie hesitated just a moment and wiped his eyes. "These people didn't deserve this," he whispered. Looking at the five graves he couldn't keep his eyes from leaking.

Lieutenant Brant patted the sergeant on his back. "No, they didn't. At least we can honor them in death with a proper burial."

Cookie sniffed and nodded before helping to unload the first casket. He and the others carried the casket across the uneven ground and gently placed it next to the first hole. The pastor came over and raised his hands over it.

"Dear Lord, we ask you to bless this soul and grant it entry into your Kingdom. May it have eternal peace and suffer no more. In Jesus' name we pray, Amen."

"Amen." The men recited in unison.

After the last body had been laid to rest, the men walked silently back toward the Wagner House. "Has anyone seen Samson?" asked Private Wilkerson.

"Come to think of it, no," replied Corporal Miller.

"Maybe we should check on him?"

"Good idea," agreed Lieutenant Brant. "The mercantile is on the way. We can make a quick stop."

As they approached the storefront, Silent Owl spoke. "Strange."

"What is the matter?" asked Wilkerson.

"The store is dark. It is the middle of the afternoon. Shouldn't it be full of customers?"

Corporal Miller bounded up the steps to the front door. "It's locked," he said jiggling the handle.

"What is going on here?"

The men spun around with their hands on their revolvers.

"Why is my store dark? And where is Samson?"

In the middle of the street stood an older man, dressed in pressed trousers and a fine shirt. A pork pie hat set atop his head.

"Mr. Katzenberger?" asked Lieutenant Brant.

"I haven't been away that long. Did you forget who I am already?"

Private Wilkerson offered his hand. "No, Sir. Let's just say we are surprised to see you."

"Why is that? I left word with Samson."

"He told us he didn't know where you were."

"And we thought you were dead," added Corporal Miller. He shifted his weight and kicked at the ground.

"What?" Mr. Katzenberger turned red as a beet. "Why would you all think such a thing?"

Private Wilkerson explained his trip into the woods with Samson, the remains they found in the sugar shack, as well as the body he and the sheriff saw on Mr. Katzenberger's back porch.

"When we found those remains, well, we thought it was you." Private Wilkerson ducked his head and shrugged.

"For the Lord's sake! I just went to Cincinnati. I travel there to sell fresh meat to a few of the hotels and restaurants there. Miss Annie always brings me something special."

"We met Miss Annie." The lieutenant approached Mr. Katzenberger. "She had three beautiful rabbits for you on the day we came to town. Since you weren't in the store, we took her home and bought them from her."

"I told Samson when I would be back. Sometimes, I don't know what goes through his head."

Silent Owl whispered to Private Wilkerson, "I told you there is something wrong about him."

The private nodded. "Mr. Katzenberger, would you say Samson has been acting strange recently?"

"He's always been a bit, odd, why do you ask?"

"You see we are investigating what killed all the people we found and believe it to be a wendigo." The lieutenant pulled out the sketch that Private Wilkerson drew of the creature's footprint.

"A what?"

Silent Owl explained about the Stonecoat and how more people may be in danger.

"I knew about the animals going missing, but people, too? I had no idea." He cleared his throat then exclaimed, "Murphy! I asked him to tend to my horses while I was away. You don't think he—"

Sheriff Nelson came over to see what the commotion was about. He stumbled as he approached the store owner. His eyes grew wide, and he sucked in a breath. "Charles, it's good to see you well."

"Sheriff, do you believe what these men are saying? A monster is killing people here in Greenville?"

"I didn't want to, but after what I've seen, it is hard to believe otherwise."

"What about Murphy? He was a good man…"

The sheriff removed his hat and placed it over his heart. "Yes, he was. The townsfolk will be most upset when they hear the news." He pitched his voice low. "I thought he was you when we found him on the back porch. He is about your height and build."

"This is all my fault! I never should have asked him to keep an eye on my house while I was away."

Private Wilkerson interjected. "No, Sir. You didn't do this. You didn't attack Murphy or anyone else. This is the work of an evil, and one we will put an end to."

Mr. Katzenberger sniffed and nodded. "I'll pay for his burial. It's the least I can do."

"The burial costs have already been taken care of," said Lieutenant Brant. "But there is something else you can help us with."

"What do you need?"

"I think it's time we paid Samson a visit."

# Chapter Sixteen

After getting directions from Mr. Katzenberger, the troop rode south toward Samson's residence. The afternoon light was fading, and Cookie expressed his concern. "Sir, do you really think we should be venturing out after dusk?"

Lieutenant Brant chuckled. "There is still plenty of light in the sky."

"Tell that to the beast that attacked me the other morning."

Silent Owl rode up to Cookie's Clydesdale. The back of his small pony barely came up to the underside of the draft horse's barrel. Corporal Miller laughed, earning a glare from Private Wilkerson.

The private watched Shaman hand Cookie something that he quickly pulled over his head and tucked into his uniform shirt.

Shaman turned his pony and rode over to Wilkerson.

"What did you give him?"

"A similar stone to the one I gave you."

"Will it protect him from the evil spirits?"

"Have you had any more visions since you wore the one I gave you?" Shaman quirked his eyebrow.

Wilkerson sighed. "Honestly, I forgot I was wearing it. You are correct. I haven't had any more visions or bad dreams come to think of it."

Silent Owl nodded.

The men came to a large two-story residence at the edge of town. It was bordered by a creek which threatened to run over its banks. The soggy ground offered little in the way of vegetation and the horses fought for balance as they slipped in the thick mud.

"Stay to the outside of the path," ordered the lieutenant.

The men obeyed, Corporal Miller following the lieutenant's horse to the left, while Wilkerson, Cookie, and Shaman stayed on the right.

As they approached the house, the front door slammed open and a blond woman wearing a blood-stained apron ran outside. "Help!" she screamed.

Corporal Miller recognized his friend from the other night. "Emily?" He quickly slid out of his saddle and wrapped the woman in his arms. "Are you alright, darling?" he asked.

Emily replied, "I am so relieved to see you. Please come quickly!"

The corporal meant to follow her back into the house, but Lieutenant Brant stopped him. "What is happening, Ma'am?" he asked her.

"It's Prudence, Sir. She is hurt something awful."

Lieutenant Brant told the corporal to go ahead and ordered the other men to set a perimeter. He followed Miller and his lady friend into the residence.

Miss Prudence lay across the floor with a gash across her chest. Deep moans permeated the candlelit room. The woman mumbled, but she didn't speak coherent words. The lieutenant knelt next to her and grasped her hand. "What is it dear?"

Her eyes fluttered up and away for a moment before they focused on him. With a haggard gasp, she wheezed, "Beast." She moved her lips to say more, but no sound came out. Her head lolled to the side and her limp hand fell away from the lieutenant's grasp.

"I'm sorry Miss. She's gone."

Corporal Miller caught his friend as she collapsed to the floor. "Emily, darling, I'm so, so sorry."

"Why?" she wailed. "Prudence was the best of us."

Lieutenant Brant paced the room and saw bloody footprints tracking toward the rear of the house. He pulled his revolver from his belt and followed the trail through the small kitchen. "Stay here!" he yelled to the corporal.

Moving slowly and cautiously, he approached the back door. Wooden fragments splintered outwards where something large and heavy must have busted through. He peered through the remains of the door. A figure stalked along the tree line that bordered the creek.

"Halt!" He bellowed. "Stop right there!" He took aim with his revolver and lined up the figure with his front sight. As his right thumb pulled the hammer down, he was tackled by something on his left.

His revolver fell out of his hand as he tumbled down the back steps. Lieutenant Brant scrambled to his knees and pulled his sabre from its scabbard. Facing the new threat, his eyes widened in surprise.

Private Wilkerson raised his arms defensively. "Sir, you were going to shoot Silent Owl!"

Lieutenant Brant looked out across the yard as Shaman walked towards him with a piece of fabric in his hand.

The lieutenant sheathed his sabre and reached for the cloth. It was a pale-yellow strip of linen with a seam and a button.

Private Wilkerson knitted his brows. "Sir, that looks like the shirt Samson was wearing."

Lieutenant Brant turned towards the house and stormed up the back steps. "What is going on here?" he demanded.

Corporal Miller and Emily rose from the Camelback sofa. Emily wiped her eyes. "Prudence was reading a passage from her Bible, like she does each day before supper. I heard her scream and ran downstairs to see what was the matter. When I found her," she looked over at her sister and her breath hitched in her chest, "I tried to help her, but there was so much blood." She sobbed, her back hunched over, and her body racked with furious tears. The corporal placed a reassuring arm around her shoulders. Once she calmed, she continued. "I heard your horses in the front yard and came running out for help." She looked again at her sister, lying dead on the floor. "You know the rest."

Lieutenant Brant asked, "Did you see or hear anything after you came down the stairs?"

Emily shook her head. "No, Sir. I was distraught." She sniffed.

"We thought this is where Samson lives." Private Wilkerson removed his hat.

"The store clerk? No, he grew up here, but hasn't stayed under this roof for a few years at least."

"And you live here with your sister?"

"Yes, all of our sisters live together."

"I thought Miss Prudence only had brothers. She didn't mention sisters when I spoke with her before." Private Wilkerson ran his hand across the top of his head.

"Oh, not blood sisters. This is a home for wayward girls. Prudence took all of us in and brought us to worship the Lord." She looked at Corporal Miller. "When we go astray, she prays extra. Oh, who will pray for me now?" Emily collapsed again into Miller's arms. He guided her back to the sofa.

"You said Samson grew up here. How is this place a girls' home if he was raised here?"

"After his family died in a fire, he had no one to care for him. Being a young lad, Prudence took him in. Treated him like he was kin. She was like that with all of us. Once he came of age, she couldn't risk his manly urges getting the better of him, so she asked him to leave. She helped him get work with Mr. Katzenberger so he could earn enough to buy his own land someday."

Lieutenant Brant offered her his hand. "Thank you, Miss Emily. You've been most helpful."

"What does any of this," she motioned around the room, "have to do with Samson? He was always an odd child, but never violent. He would never harm a fly."

"We just have some questions for him. If you see him, can you let him know to come find us?"

"Find you? Oh no, I am not staying here tonight. I'm coming with you back to the Wagner House." She stamped her foot.

Corporal Miller shrugged his shoulders and looked at the lieutenant.

Cookie pointed out the window. "It is getting dark, Sir."

Lieutenant Brant sighed. "Very well. Miss Emily, gather your things. Cookie, find a sheet for Miss Prudence. Private Wilkerson and Silent Owl, please ride to Sheriff Nelson's office. And take this with you." He handed Wilkerson the scrap of fabric. "It looks like we have another body for the undertaker."

Private Wilkerson placed the frayed linen into a pocket and mounted Dawson. He and Shaman's war pony trotted the length of town in time to reach the sheriff's office at dusk. David rapped on the door, but there was no answer. He started around the back of the building and stopped short at Silent Owl's yell.

David turned in time to face a sallow-colored beast with pale yellow eyes. Its long snout sniffed at him, skin stretched so thin over its skull, that it resembled the hide covering a drum. Long fangs dripped with saliva and its claws left scratches on the porch as it stalked closer. The creature snarled at him and opened its maw wide.

Wilkerson reached for his revolvers and pulled them free of his belt. He lowered his hips and stood in a deep stance. Thumbing the hammers back, he heard the comforting whirr of the cylinder as it clicked a cartridge in line with the barrel.

The creature snarled again and leaped into the air. Its claws stretched toward him and clawed through the space between them as it flew closer and closer.

David jerked both triggers and the revolvers jumped in his hands as the lead flew true.

*Boom!* His ears rang and he could taste the chalky grit of gunpowder on his tongue. Blood blossomed on the creature's chest. As the beast staggered, Wilkerson thumbed the hammers and fired again, hoping for a killing blow. His heart hammered in his chest as the beast fought to stay upright. After what felt like an eternity, it collapsed. David took a shuddering breath, his hands shaking with the weight of his weapons, but he didn't dare lower them. Not yet.

The creature struggled against the ground, trying to right itself. It huffed as it clawed at the dirt, pulling itself inches closer to Wilkerson.

David backed away, his weapons trained on the creature's face. Out of the corner of his eye, he saw Silent Owl stalking toward them with his tomahawk raised.

The beast turned its head toward the Shaman and then stilled. Its ghostly yellow eyes dimmed as it stared blankly into the star-filled sky.

Wilkerson moved over to Silent Owl, keeping his revolvers pointed at the threat.

Shaman moved towards the creature and kicked it with a moccasin-covered foot. It didn't move.

David kept an eye on the beast and only turned away when he heard a voice behind him.

"What in tarnation?"

"Sheriff, I'm glad to see you." David placed his revolvers back in his belt.

"Wish I could say the same, Son. What is that thing?" The sheriff pointed at the slain creature.

Silent Owl walked over to them. "It appears to be a Stonecoat, but not."

"Not?" asked Wilkerson.

"Your bullets killed it. Stonecoats are not harmed by guns or blades. Also, look at its head. There are no antlers. This creature looks like a Stonecoat, but different."

"Maybe this is one of the people the wendigo conscripted?" asked David.

"Conscripted?" asked the sheriff. "Are you saying there is more than one of these things in my town?"

"I don't know, Sir." Wilkerson walked closer to the beast. As he approached, the creature's form changed and shifted. David jumped backward a pace and pulled his revolver.

The elongated snout shrank into its face and a human-looking nose emerged. Its fearsome claws shortened into fingernails. Ears sprouted on each side of its head.

David turned the beast onto its back, and where a hideous creature had lain a moment before, now was a skeletal young man.

Sheriff Nelson walked over to the body. "Son, if I hadn't seen that thing before now, I'd be locking you away for murder." He whistled. "Although," he peered at the man's face, "he looks a mite bit familiar."

David looked closer. Dark hair appeared on the young man's head. His skin color changed from sallow to a pasty white. "Sure does, Sheriff. Isn't that Samson?"

The sheriff removed his hat. "Aw, heck! He was a good kid, bit odd, but a good kid none the less."

"I'm sorry Sheriff." Wilkerson placed a hand on the older man's shoulder.

"Don't be Son. It looks to me like you were just defending yourself."

"That's true enough. I just never killed anyone before." David's voice cracked and his breath hitched in his chest. He broke away from the sheriff's gaze to observe the blood-stained ground at their feet.

The sheriff regarded him with a sympathetic eye. "Let's go visit the undertaker again."

"That's actually why we came to see you in the first place."

The sheriff raised an eyebrow at him.

"We need the undertaker for two bodies tonight."

Silent Owl stayed with Samson's body while the sheriff and Private Wilkerson walked to the undertaker's office. The night was crisp and cool with a bright moon hanging in the sky.

Sheriff Nelson knocked on the door and the undertaker answered. "We are in need of your services again."

"Again? I still haven't finished the caskets for the other bodies you found."

"I'm not happy about this either," grumbled the sheriff.

The undertaker gave Private Wilkerson a sidelong glance before waving both men inside. "You should know the way by now."

They walked through the back room where another dozen caskets were in various stages of construction. Private Wilkerson marveled at the craftsmanship of each one. "I didn't get to fully appreciate your work this morning. These are lovely."

The undertaker sniffed. "I would thank you; however, I do not appreciate the extra practice my family and I have had lately."

Private Wilkerson opened his mouth to reply but thought better of it. He closed his jaw with a click and clenched his teeth.

"If you're done admiring my handiwork?" The undertaker pointed to his wagon.

Private Wilkerson sat between the undertaker and Sheriff Nelson in uncomfortable silence. He wanted to say something, anything, but what could he say? It wasn't his fault the wendigo was attacking these people. He didn't agree to join Red's "master" so why did he feel so guilty? And where was Red? Would he turn into the same type of creature as Samson? Would David have to shoot his best childhood friend to save his own life? He shook his head as the wagon approached the sheriff's office.

The men climbed off the buckboard and surrounded Samson's body. They lifted him gently into the back. As the undertaker wrapped him in a sheet, he said. "How long ago did he die?"

"No more than the ten minutes it took us to fetch you and get back here." The sheriff wiped his brow.

"Why do you ask?" David's heart rate increased. His mouth grew dry. The last thing he needed was for the undertaker to think him a cold-blooded killer. He was trying to help find the cause of all these deaths, not add to the body count.

"Feel his skin." The undertaker pulled back the sheet to reveal Samson's chest.

The sheriff touched the middle of his chest. "He feels like the surface of the lake in the middle of winter."

David reached up and felt the dead man's skin, as well. "He's only been gone a few minutes. How'd he get so cold, so fast?"

"Check his heart." Silent Owl peered at them from behind. "Legend says the Stonecoat has a chunk of ice where its heart should be." He pulled one of his knives out of his breechcloth and took a step closer to Samson's still form.

"I won't have you desecrating the body!" The sheriff hollered. "Let's have some respect for the dead."

"While I would normally agree with you, Sheriff, he wasn't exactly human when he passed. He didn't change until after." David looked at his boots.

"Changed how? What are you all talking about?" The undertaker was getting more upset by the moment.

"Please, let me check." Silent Owl placed the blade of his knife in his teeth and hopped into the back of the wagon. He felt Samson's body on the left side of his chest and lowered his head. After saying a silent prayer, he plunged the knife between two ribs and into his heart.

The men outside braced themselves for a gory scene. David panted and clenched his teeth to keep from vomiting.

Silent Owl lifted the knife slowly from the body. Instead of a red trail of liquid, water droplets spilled from the blade. "It is as I thought. There is no blood."

The undertaker jumped up in the wagon next to him. He reached his finger inside the wound to check for himself. When he pulled his hand away, shards of ice clung to his skin.

"Okay fellas, I don't know what in Hell is going on here, and I don't want to. I'm going to take this boy back to my place and get him prepped for burial. Ya'll have a good night."

"Not so fast," the sheriff said. He looked at Wilkerson. "You said there was another body?"

"Yes, Sheriff." David untied Dawson from the hitching post and mounted up. "Follow me and I'll show you where."

The undertaker grumbled something under his breath and jumped into the driver's seat.

Wilkerson and Shaman led the wagon across town and back to the home of Miss Prudence and her sisters. David led them through the threshold to where her body lay.

Cookie was kneeling next to her with his elbows at his sides and hands clasped in prayer.

"Sergeant?" Wilkerson approached him slowly.

Cookie cleared his throat. "I was just saying a few words."

"Of course. Where are the others?"

"Miss Emily couldn't stay here any longer, so Lieutenant Brant and Corporal Miller escorted her back to the Wagner House. I didn't want Miss Prudence to be alone, so I stayed with her until you all came back."

"What about the other girls? Do we need accommodations for the other sisters?"

"Miss Emily didn't mention anyone else. I'm not certain." Cookie stood and stretched.

"Sheriff? Do you know if anyone else lives here?"

"Most of the other girls have grown up and moved away. As far as I know, only Prudence and Emily do."

"The other night, there were three more ladies with them. They don't live here, too?"

The sheriff chuckled. "No, those other ladies are members of the Church. When Miss Prudence gets an idea about something, the others all tend to follow suit." He sobered. "I will need to tell them what happened." He sighed.

"I almost forgot." Private Wilkerson fished out the scrap of fabric from his pocket. "Lieutenant Brant found this. He thinks it might belong to whoever or whatever attacked her."

The sheriff picked the fabric out of Wilkerson's hand and held it to the light. "Looks to me like part of a man's shirt."

"That is what we thought." Private Wilkerson looked at Cookie.

Cookie asked, "Any idea who that shirt might belong to?"

The sheriff sighed again. "I think it belongs to the man you shot behind my office."

Cookie bristled. "What happened?"

Private Wilkerson shared the events from earlier in the evening.

"How are you holding up?" Cookie looked intently at the private.

"I'll be better once we get to the bottom of this."

"And I'll be better once I can get home to supper." The undertaker stood in the doorway with his arms crossed over his chest.

The sheriff, sergeant, private, and Shaman helped the undertaker load Prudence's body into the wagon. "Sheriff, did you want to take a look around?"

"Let's wait until daylight. Besides, my ride is leaving without me." He hustled to the wagon and scrambled onto the buckboard as the undertaker flicked the reins over his horses' backs.

"We should probably head back, too," Wilkerson said to Cookie.

"That's the best idea you've had yet."

# Chapter Seventeen

Private Wilkerson rode Dawson back to the livery in silence. He couldn't help but relive the horror of watching that creature turn back into Samson's form. He shuddered involuntarily as he swung his leg over his horse's back to dismount.

"Do you want me to take care of him tonight?" The livery boy asked with a sheepish smile.

"Thank you, but no, I could use a friend and he's the best one I have at the moment. No offense."

"None taken." The boy handed Wilkerson a brush and went to fetch forage and a bucket of oats.

"Would you like me to remain with you?" Silent Owl took the rope away from his horse's neck and she followed him into one of the stalls.

"No, I think I need to be alone for a while."

"Are you sure that's a good idea?" Cookie asked. "You've had quite the day."

"I'm certain, just save me some whiskey, will ya?"

Cookie chuckled and followed Silent Owl out of the barn.

David uncinched the buckle on his girth and lifted the saddle over Dawson's withers. Despite the chill in the air, sweat foamed where the pad and girth rubbed the horse's brown coat. Wilkerson wiped the sweaty spots with a rag and Dawson leaned into his touch. "Feels good, doesn't it boy?"

Dawson turned his thick neck and rubbed his forehead along David's left shoulder. White hairs from the star on his face drifted in the air, catching the rays of light from a lamp hanging from the rafters.

Wilkerson swatted the hairs away from his face, but it was too late. He sneezed.

Dawson nickered and tossed his head.

"Glad you thought that was funny." Despite his runny nose, he couldn't help but smile.

After he finished grooming his horse and oiling his tack, he headed across the street to the Wagner House. A cool breeze ruffled his hair and carried a shrill sound to his ear.

David stopped, his heart in his throat. Swallowing, he gripped the disc of obsidian hanging around his neck. Since Shaman had given it to him, he hadn't had any vivid dreams. Red didn't visit him anymore. So, what had him so worked up?

He looked warily down both sides of the street. Seeing nothing out of the ordinary, he took a cautious step and released the breath he didn't realize he had been holding.

As soon as his hand touched the knob of the Wagner House front door, a sharp note pierced the silence. Wilkerson dropped his hand to his waist and spun around to face the threat, the grip of his revolver within reach.

"I didn't mean to startle you, Son."

"Sheriff Nelson?"

The sheriff nodded. "I guess you're pretty worked up over what happened earlier today."

"You could say that."

"Come inside, I'll buy you a drink."

"I'd appreciate that, Sir."

Silent Owl glared as the sheriff entered the dining room. The Spirits told him to be wary with this one, just as they had warned about the store clerk, Samson. Whereas Samson walked between worlds, this Sheriff was different. There was a darkness about him the Shaman could not place, and that worried him. He was coming to appreciate the companionship of young Private David Wilkerson and didn't want to see any harm come to him. Silent Owl would have to remain vigilant.

As David and the sheriff approached the bar, Silent Owl stood. "Can I have a word with you?"

"Of course." David pulled out a barstool.

"In private." Shaman arched his eyebrows at the sheriff.

Sheriff Nelson just nodded and waved at Herr Wagner for a drink.

Wilkerson pushed the stool back against the bar.

Shaman walked toward the door with David in tow. As they reached the threshold, Wilkerson asked, "Why outside?"

"Why not? It is a nice night."

David rolled his shoulders back and puffed out his chest as he walked through the doorway.

"Tell me what happened?"

"You know what happened. You were there!" David's face flushed.

"That is not what I mean. Just now. What happened when you were with the horses?"

"Nothing. The obsidian disc you gave me must still work." Wilkerson swallowed hard. "I'll admit I thought I heard something when I was leaving the barn, but it must just have been my imagination."

"There is more. Tell me everything."

David shrugged. "When I went to go inside, the sheriff startled me."

"How did he do that?"

"I was on edge from thinking about Red and wondering if he was going to show up again, and I wasn't paying attention to my surroundings. I thought I heard something behind me, but it was just the sheriff."

"What did you think you heard?"

"Just someone whistling, that's all. Like I said, my nerves were on edge. It wasn't anything."

Silent Owl stared at him expressionlessly.

"I mean it. Can we go have a drink now?"

Shaman nodded, then said, "Please be careful around the sheriff. There is something about him I do not trust."

"Why? He's the law. Why wouldn't you trust him?"

"A shiny piece of metal does not a good man make."

Private Wilkerson walked back inside and saw Corporal Miller and Emily seated at a table for two. He grabbed a whiskey and walked over to them.

"How are you holding up?"

Emily turned to him with red-rimmed eyes. "I don't know what I'm going to do. Without Prudence, that house just won't be home. I can't go back there. Every time I think about it, I can't help but see her lying there on the floor." She gasped.

Miller grabbed her hand and wrapped his other arm around her shoulder. "It'll be alright. You don't have to make any decisions tonight."

Emily looked at Wilkerson's drink and threw her hands into the air. "What is the matter with you?"

David stared at her. "What do you mean?"

"My sister is dead, and you honor her memory by drinking whiskey? You should be ashamed of yourself!" She stood abruptly and stormed up the stairs.

Corporal Miller pushed his chair back. "She is on edge. Give her some time and I'm sure she'll calm down. Enjoy your drink. I'll see you in the morning."

With that, he followed Emily to his room.

Private Wilkerson sat at the abandoned table and hung his head to his chest. He just couldn't catch a break today.

Sheriff Nelson approached and pointed to the other chair. David nodded. As the sheriff sat, Wilkerson saw Silent Owl staring at them from across the room. He sighed.

"What has you all hot and bothered?" The sheriff took a sip from his whiskey glass.

"It's been a long day, and we still don't know what we're dealing with. People are dropping like flies. How are we supposed to stop the killings if we don't know how many monsters are out there, or even what they look like?"

The sheriff leaned forward. "Not all the problems of the world can fit on your shoulders. Shake off some of those burdens. You have plenty of help." He pointed at Lieutenant Brant and Cookie as they visited with Herr Wagner. "Besides, tomorrow is another day." He squeezed David's shoulder and headed over to the bar, Shaman glaring at him the entire time.

Wilkerson downed his glass and went to bed. The sheriff was right. A new day would begin with the dawn.

Lieutenant Brant watched Private Wilkerson walk upstairs then turned his attention to his half-empty glass. Cookie told tall tales while Herr Wagner roared with laughter. Despite the jovial company, he just couldn't join in.

Sheriff Nelson pulled up the stool next to him. "Lieutenant?"

"Hello again, Sheriff. I apologize for my private causing you more work."

"I'm not. If it wasn't for Wilkerson, I would never have known about Samson. To think that boy was killing and eating people right under my nose. How could I not see it?" He reached for the bottle on the bar.

Lieutenant Brant stayed his hand. "If you don't mind my saying, maybe we should slow down tonight. Tomorrow, I'd like my men to accompany you back to Miss Prudence's place. Maybe we can find out more about the beast that attacked her."

The sheriff nodded. "I'll meet you there in the morning." He stood to leave.

"Sheriff?"

"Something else?"

"How about you join us for breakfast? My treat."

"I'm not one to turn down a free meal. See you at first light." The sheriff tipped his hat and turned on his heel. No sooner did his backside clear the doorway, than Silent Owl swooped to the barstool he had just vacated.

"What can I do for you, Shaman?" Lieutenant Brant drained his glass and pushed it away.

"There is something wrong about Sheriff Nelson."

"Wrong how?"

"I do not know, just a darkness in his soul I can't describe."

"He's the law, and I'm sure he's seen things that would make us quake in our boots."

"Be that as it may, I do not trust him."

"As always, Silent Owl, I appreciate your insight. Your expertise was instrumental with that band of Comanche, and I trust your instincts. Right now, there is nothing we can do about the sheriff but keep a wary eye. For now, let's call it a night. Tomorrow, we'll head back to where Miss Prudence was killed and see if we can get a better idea of what we're dealing with."

"Emily, I need your help. Emily!"

Emily sat bolt upright in Corporal Miller's bed. Her heart hammered in her chest and her body quaked with fear. She reached for a lamp on the nightstand with a shaking hand.

"No, no light. It burns."

"Prudence?" Emily whispered.

A disembodied voice crossed the room. "Yes. I'm here and I need you to do something for me."

"Anything. How are you speaking to me? I thought you were dead."

"My body is gone, but my soul remains. I need you to find my Bible and bring it to the undertaker. I need it buried with me, or my soul will be stranded here."

"I—I can't. I can't go back there." Emily's body involuntarily shook. The movement knocked the lamp onto the floor.

Corporal Miller turned over in his sleep and reached for her.

Emily held her breath and placed a pillow under his arm.

Miller rolled next to the pillow and squeezed it.

Emily waited until she heard him snoring softly before she spoke again. "Prudence, I would do anything for you, but I'm frightened. I can't bear the thought of seeing you lying on the floor like that again."

"You won't, I promise. My body is with the undertaker. I just need you to bring my Bible."

"I don't know…" Tears dripped down her face. "It's dark out!" She protested. "Can it wait until morning?"

"Emily! Does my soul mean that little to you? You would deny me my place in Paradise because of your fear?"

Emily gasped. "No!" She remembered herself and whispered, "For God has not given us a spirit of fear, but of power and of love and of a sound mind."

"That's right."

Emily steeled herself. "I will do this for you, but I'm not going alone. Let me wake Ethan."

"No! You must come alone. Ethan Miller doesn't understand our beliefs. He will make you wait until morning, and it will be too late."

"But—" Emily held her face in her hands.

"I don't have much time. Now please, hurry!"

Prudence's voice faded into the darkness. Emily thought she must be dreaming until she heard Corporal Miller breathing beside her. She leaned down to give him a soft peck on the cheek before getting out of bed.

She dressed quickly and headed out into the night.

The walk across town took all the faith Emily had within her. Each sound caused her fear to spike, and she almost turned back a half-dozen times. Praying the whole way there, Emily finally approached the house she had shared with her sister and paused. Prudence said this was important, and she certainly didn't want to be the one to deny her sister's place with the Lord. Yet, something felt wrong.

"Emily? You came? Thank you!"

Hearing her sister's voice again calmed her nerves and filled her with resolve. She squared her shoulders and walked up the front steps. The door was unlocked; in her despair, she must have forgotten to secure the door. Then she remembered Prudence's body was still inside when she left with Miller and the lieutenant.

"Prudence?"

"Yes, dear. I'm right here. My Bible is on the table where I always keep it." Her voice echoed in the empty house.

Emily tip-toed through the darkness and found the table. Her fingers brushed the leather cover when she felt something behind her. She turned and looked straight into a skeletal chest. "You're not Prudence!" Emily gasped.

A gravelly voice responded, "No.... I needed you to come back here so I could finish what I started with your sister."

"Help!" She opened her mouth to scream but no sound came out. Her heart skipped a beat. Emily's hands went numb, and she tried to move away from the beast. Her legs turned to jelly, and she froze in place. Tears leaked out of her wide eyes as she gazed into her fate.

The beast grabbed her about the throat and squeezed. Emily flailed about in the creature's grasp to no avail. The last thing she saw were the gilded letters of her sister's Bible illuminated by moonlight.

Lieutenant Brant rose before the sun. He stood and stretched his arms down to his toes to work out the kinks in his back. At his age, he should appreciate sleeping in a proper bed, but after all his years in the cavalry, he yearned to sleep on the ground underneath the stars. *I should be careful what I wish for. Once we slay this Stonecoat, or wendigo, or whatever it is, we'll be sleeping in camps soon enough.* "At least I hope."

A soft knock on his door announced the arrival of a courier. Brant greeted the young lad and handed him a three-cent nickel.

"Th-thank you, Sir!" The boy stammered and bounded down the stairs.

Brant took the note back inside his room and closed the wooden door. It read:

*Reinforcements incoming. Whatever you do, do not leave Greenville until they arrive. We have reports of similar attacks all throughout the western territories. Stay vigilant!*

*Captain McLellan*

Lieutenant Brant sighed. Reinforcements were good, but how many men were they sending? What equipment would they have, and would it be enough to stop the Stonecoat of Silent Owl's legend? Another knock interrupted his thoughts.

"Enter," he called.

"Morning, Sir," Corporal Miller offered the lieutenant a crisp salute.

"What can I do for you, Corporal?"

"It's Miss Emily, Sir. She stayed with me last night, but now she's gone."

"Perhaps she went to wash up, or get some coffee?"

"I thought of that, Sir. Herr Wagner hasn't seen her since she came up to my room last evening. I checked the kitchen and even went out to the livery. There is no sign of her."

"I'm sure she'll turn up. Don't fret."

"After what happened to her sister, how can I not?"

"Maybe she went back to the house?"

"I doubt that, Sir. She was just telling Wilkerson last night that she couldn't possibly go back there after what happened."

"We will know soon enough. Let's eat,then we will head over to the house and continue our mission."

"But Sir—"

"That is an order, Corporal."

"Yes, Sir."

Private Wilkerson splashed cool water on his face. He stared at his reflection in the basin. Yesterday, he was a cavalry private, on a mission to keep order in a town with a women's crusade against liquor. That all changed when he had to shoot a man, although the man wasn't exactly human when he attacked him. As he regarded the visage in the pool of water, his hair lightened from brown to red. Freckles emerged on his nose and his eyes took on a yellow tint. He thrust the wash basin away, water splashing his arms and soaking through his uniform shirt.

He shivered and bent over to retrieve the shattered basin from the floor.

"Everything alright in there?" A soft knock followed the female voice.

David crossed the room and opened the door. "Yes, Miss. Sorry for the commotion."

The serving girl from the dining room peered under his arm and noticed the small puddle in the corner of the room. "I'll go fetch you some towels." As she spied the fragment of the basin in his hand, she added, "And a new wash basin."

Wilkerson's cheeks burned in embarrassment. "It's okay, I can clean up after myself."

"No trouble at all, I promise."

"I thought you worked downstairs."

The girl blushed. "I did. Herr Wagner complained about all the broken dishes and wasted food, so he moved me to housekeeping." She shrugged, then shot a wink over her shoulder as she turned away.

David's heart fluttered in his chest. He changed into a dry shirt and left the wet one on the bed. In his hurry, he didn't realize the obsidian disc Silent Owl gave him clattered to the floor. As soon as he made his way to the door, the girl was there with fresh towels.

"I hope you don't mind, but I have a shirt that needs washing."

She smiled at him. "No trouble. It'll be ready for you tomorrow."

He filed past her and headed down to breakfast.

With full bellies and a purpose in their hearts, the men headed back to Miss Prudence's house. Cookie tried to lighten the mood, but Sheriff Nelson stopped him with a glare. "Sergeant, I appreciate what you are doing, but there is a time and a place for revelry. I'm afraid this is neither the time nor the place."

Cookie nodded and rode silently with a glum expression on his face.

Silent Owl rode next to Private Wilkerson between him and the sheriff. He seemed determined to keep the Sheriff away from David, but why? David shook his head.

The sheriff helped them with the bodies they found. He showed them where Mr. Katzenberger lived and even helped them with the corpses they found in the sugar shack. David couldn't understand why Shaman had reservations about the sheriff. He made to ask, but Silent Owl shushed him and closed his eyes.

Shaman's lips moved as he rode along the street and didn't stop until they reached the residence.

"What are you doing?" David asked him.

"The Spirits and I are conversing. Even though you left your amulet behind, they are still with you."

"What do you—" David reached into his shirt for the obsidian disc and felt nothing. He wiped his hand along the back of his neck, but the leather cord wasn't there either. "Dammit!"

"What is the problem?" asked Corporal Miller.

"I lost my amulet."

"You believe in that mumbo jumbo?" The corporal looked at Silent Owl. "No offense."

"None taken. You pale faces do not understand half of the world around you." He shook his head and rode up to where Lieutenant Brant and Sheriff Nelson were tying their horses.

"Why do you have to be like that?"

"Like what?" The corporal thrust his right arm out toward Wilkerson.

"Shaman is just trying to help us. Since he gave me that 'mumbo jumbo' I haven't had any more weird dreams. I think it really worked."

Corporal Miller tapped his temple with his trigger finger. "It's all in your head."

David huffed and rode away.

After they dismounted and checked their weapons, Lieutenant Brant called a quick meeting. "Men, I received a telegram this morning."

"And you didn't tell us that before now?" Corporal Miler groused.

"*Corporal,* I realize you are worried about your lady friend, but I will expect you to watch your tone. I am still your commanding officer."

"What did the telegram say, Sir?" Wilkerson asked to take the attention from the corporal.

"We are receiving reinforcements."

"Are they sending artillery?" Cookie rubbed his hands together excitedly.

"Like you would know what to do with a Parrott Gun." Miller grinned.

Cookie glared at the corporal. "I wasn't always a Supply Sergeant." He huffed and turned his attention back to the lieutenant.

"The note didn't state, just that we are to stay here in Greenville until they arrive, and to 'stay vigilant.'" Lieutenant Brant turned his attention to the house.

"So, what do we do until they get here?" asked the corporal, with a respectful tone this time.

"We keep doing what we've been doing. We work with the Sheriff," the lieutenant pointed at Nelson, "and try to figure out what we're dealing with. Once we know what exactly the monster is, we can relay that information to the rest of our Special Unit when they get here.

"In the meantime, let's take the sheriff's lead. Where do you want us to start?"

Sheriff Nelson led the troop across the front yard of Miss Prudence's house. "Sergeant Taylor, I want you and Silent Owl to watch the tree line along the back of the property. Walk through the woods and let me know if you see any tracks or anything else that might tell us more about what attacked Miss Prudence.

"Lieutenant Brant and Corporal Miller, please stay in the front of the house. The townsfolk are sure to question what we're doing here and ask about Miss Prudence. Let them know I will answer their questions in due time, but they need to be patient.

"Private Wilkerson, you're with me."

Silent Owl made to protest, but the lieutenant held up a hand.

"We're in his town, and we will follow his lead. This is his investigation, do you understand?"

Silent Owl grumbled but nodded in assent.

"As I was saying, Private, you and I will stay inside the house and see what we can find."

The men disbursed to tackle their assignments. Once they were alone, the sheriff leaned toward David. "So, tell me more about what happened with the creature who used to be Samson."

"There's not much to tell, Sheriff. Silent Owl and I came to your office to tell you what happened to Miss Prudence. Your office was dark, so I went to walk around to see if you were in the back. I heard a yell, and when I turned around that beast attacked me. I had no choice but to shoot it. Like you said, it was self-defense."

The sheriff whistled. "Are you sure you didn't do anything to provoke it?"

"Pardon me? With respect, Sheriff, I was just walking when it came up on me!"

"So you said, I'm just verifying your story." The sheriff turned away and walked up the stairs.

David sighed. He stepped carefully around the red puddle in the middle of the room. Scratches marred the surface of the rug. Bending down, he traced his finger along one jagged tear. There was another about a foot and a half away. He followed the trail of rips across the floor and ended up next to the back door. Examining the destroyed wood, he peered through the hole. Silent Owl and Cookie traipsed along the wood line.

Wilkerson turned around and headed into the kitchen. Droplets of blood spattered along the trail of claw marks, but he didn't find anything else of interest.

*What are we doing here? We aren't inspectors. We're cavalrymen. How are we supposed to help the sheriff find out what killed Prudence?*

He sighed again and walked over to the sofa. As he sat, something in the corner of the floor caught his eye. David walked across the room and found a tattered pile of clothing.

"Sheriff!"

Sheriff Nelson ran down the stairs. "What is it?"

"I think I found something."

The Sheriff picked up an item on top of the heap and held it up. "What does this look like to you?"

"It looks like a faded shirt, or at least pieces of it."

"I wonder," the Sheriff reached into his shirt pocket and pulled out the scrap of fabric David gave him yesterday, "if this is where this piece came from."

He laid the shredded garment on the table next to Prudence's Bible and placed the fabric scrap on top.

As David watched, the pieces lined up. "What does this mean, Sheriff?"

"This means Samson, or the beast he turned into, killed Miss Prudence."

"Now what do we do?"

"Look for anything else he might have left behind."

Wilkerson scanned the room but didn't see anything of consequence. "I don't know what I'm looking for."

The back door opened with a creak. "Private, go get the Lieutenant." Cookie cleared his throat and pointed to the front of the house. His arm quivered and sweat beaded on his forehead.

"Cookie, what happened?"

The sergeant swallowed hard. "Go. Now."

David had never seen Cookie this upset, so he did as the Sergeant ordered with no further questions.

Lieutenant Brant and Corporal Miller followed him back through the house and into the rear yard.

"What do you have Sergeant?" Lieutenant Brant asked.

Cookie's face went ashen as he pointed up into a large oak tree.

The men followed his gaze and saw a female form lying across a low-hanging branch. Blond hair hung limp from her head and her blue eyes stared lifelessly at the ground. Blood trailed down the trunk of the tree and pooled at its base. Steam billowed from the puddle and drifted away into the nearby fog.

"Emily!" Corporal Miller shouted and fell to his knees. He pounded at the frozen ground. "Why? Why would you come back here by yourself?" He wailed. Tears streamed down his face. His breath came in haggard gasps as he shouted. "I could have come with you! If I had been here—"

Silent Owl pulled the corporal to his feet. "If you had been here, the Stonecoat would have killed you as well."

"Then I should be dead with her." The corporal sniffed. He turned toward Emily's body.

"No. Remember her how she was. Not like this." Shaman escorted Miller back inside.

"That's a damn shame." Sheriff Nelson removed his hat and bowed his head.

Lieutenant Brant said a small prayer. "Private, go fetch the undertaker. Cookie and I will get her down."

"What's the point, Sir? People are getting killed right under our noses. I shot Samson yesterday, and for what? Emily was alive last night after the undertaker took the creature's body. How many more people have to die?"

Lieutenant Brant looked sternly into David's eyes. "I realize you didn't sign up for this, but this is the hand we've been dealt. Obviously, there is still at least one other monster here preying on this town. Right now, we have to take care of Miss Emily. After that, we will figure out the rest. Now git!"

Wilkerson squared his shoulders and ran to his horse.

Despite the morning sun, Wilkerson shivered in the saddle as he rode across town. A low mist filled the street making it difficult for him to see where he was going. After what felt like an eternity, he knocked on the undertaker's door.

"You again?"

"It's Miss Emily. We need your services."

The undertaker slammed the door in David's face. From the other side, Wilkerson heard, "I know the way. We were just there last night for God's sake."

"I'll meet you there." Wilkerson turned back to his mount.

"Lucky me…" The undertaker's muffled voice replied.

*I know the feeling.* Private Wilkerson rode back across town. The mist thickened into fog as soon as he reached the house where Prudence and Emily had lived. *Who will live here now?* he wondered.

As he pulled Dawson to a stop, the horse reared up and let out a shrill whinny.

"What's wrong, Boy?" David leaned forward in the saddle and patted Dawson's right wither. Holding the reins in his left hand, he scanned for whatever it was that spooked his mount.

A shrill whistle came from the fog. A glowing set of yellow eyes emerged from the mist. Wilkerson squeezed Dawson with his legs and the horse brought his front hooves back to the ground.

David pulled his revolver from his belt and took aim. "What do you want?"

The eyes came closer and coalesced into another hideous creature with a skeletal frame, taut skin, sharp claws, and long fangs. Unlike Samson, this one had a patch of red hair on the top of its head.

Wilkerson lowered his weapon. "Red, is that you?"

The creature stalked forward on all fours but hesitated when David said the name.

Wilkerson tried again. "Private Aiden Flanagan."

The creature stopped and looked at him. It sat on its rear haunches like a dog waiting for table scraps.

"It is you, isn't it?"

Just then, the undertaker's wagon trundled up the road. David turned towards the sound to warn the driver. "Don't stop; keep moving!"

The undertaker shook his head and pulled back on the reins. "Would you make up your mind? Do you want help with Miss Emily or don't you?"

"But the creature—"

"What creature? Ain't nothing here but you and your horse." The undertaker waved his arm around.

Wilkerson looked back toward Red, and sure enough, he was gone. Gone too was the fog that had filled the front yard a moment ago.

"You need to have your head examined." The undertaker drove around the back of the house.

*How does he know where to go? I never told him where to find Miss Emily's body...*

David shook his head and dismounted. He joined the rest of the men in the backyard.

Corporal Miller stood over Emily's body. A blood-stained sheet covered her form. His eyes were red, and his hands clenched into fists.

Wilkerson walked up to him and patted him on the shoulder. "I'm sorry."

"So am I. After this mission, I was going to ask her to leave this town and start a life with me." Fresh tears flowed down his face. He sniffed and looked at the private. "So help me, we're gonna find the thing that killed her, and it'll be the last thing that beast ever does. You mark my words." Miller stared out into the distance.

David nodded, not knowing what to say. Instead, he approached Silent Owl.

"How is your friend?"

"You tell me. You were with him while I was gone."

"Not the corporal. How is Red?"

"How do you know about that?"

"The Spirits tell me things." Shaman shrugged.

Wilkerson leaned into Shaman and whispered, "He was here just a moment ago, at least I think it was him. I rode back from the undertaker's office and when I got here, there was a creature in the fog waiting for me. It looked like Samson, but it had a patch of red hair on its head. When I said Red's name, it stopped."

"Hmm… Legend says that a human turned wendigo will remember their friends and family after they turn."

"Does that mean he won't try to attack me again?"

"I know not."

"You're a big help."

Shaman shrugged again. "To be safe, we need to get your amulet."

Wilkerson nodded. "It must be back at the Wagner House. I wore it to sleep last night and didn't take it off."

He remembered seeing Red's face in his reflection from the wash basin. *In my rush to take off my wet shirt, I must have also taken off the amulet.* "As soon as we're done here, I'm sure that will be our next stop."

Silent Owl and the private joined the men surrounding Miss Emily. They lifted her into the undertaker's wagon.

"It's such a pleasure doing business with you," the undertaker said dryly.

Sheriff Nelson muttered something under his breath as the undertaker drove away. He looked at Corporal Miller. "With Miss Prudence gone, Emily doesn't have any kin."

"I'll take care of her burial, Sheriff." Corporal Miller sniffed.

The Sheriff placed his hand on the corporal's shoulder. "We'll find what did this."

"I'm not leaving this town until we do."

# Chapter Eighteen

The men rode back to the Wagner House in silence. Even the horses seemed somber with a slow gait and heads drooping. Instead of fighting the bit back to the livery, Wilkerson had to keep leg pressure on Dawson's sides to keep him moving forward. "Hey, Cookie! Is your horse alright?"

"What do you mean, Private?"

"Last night, Dawson couldn't wait to get back to the barn, but now it's like he's hesitating."

"Come to think of it, Beau is plodding along, too." Corporal Miller patted his mount. "I thought he was just picking up on my mood."

Lieutenant Brant called a halt. "Eyes up. The horses can sense things we cannot. Pay attention and be wary."

Silent Owl maneuvered his war pony to the back of the group.

Cookie took point with the lieutenant and corporal behind him and to his left and right. Wilkerson rode behind them and in front of Shaman.

As they got closer to the Wagner House, dusk descended. Fog floated around and between them. A chill breeze ruffled their horses' manes.

"Isn't it a mite early for nightfall?" Cookie's voice cracked.

"Stand tall, Sergeant," Lieutenant Brant ordered.

At the sound of his confident voice, all the men sat straighter in their saddles. They scanned their surroundings for any sign of trouble.

And trouble they found.

Scattered around the front of the Wagner House was a group of no less than seventy ladies kneeling in prayer. They held their Bibles and sang hymns in the middle of the street.

Lieutenant Brant rode over to the hitching post, weaving between the gathered souls, and dismounted. He tipped his hat. "Ladies."

One of them stood and marched over to him. "I certainly hope a man of your caliber doesn't plan on partaking of the unholy liquor tonight."

"Unholy, you say? Why is that?"

"Libations are the swill of the Devil. It opens the drinker to the temptations of the flesh."

"Ma'am I can assure you I have never done anything drunk that I wouldn't do sober."

She looked as if he had struck her in the face. "Well, I never!" The woman gathered up her skirts and went back to her spot in the dirt. She glared at the lieutenant before bowing her head.

Private Wilkerson rode over and took the reins from the lieutenant's hand. "I will get your horse put up for the night."

"Thank you, Private. Be sure to keep your wits about you." He gestured at the group of women blocking the street. "Lord knows what they have planned tonight."

"Yes, Sir."

David led the horses into the livery. Corporal Miller, Cookie, and Silent Owl followed with theirs. Wilkerson looked at the corporal. "I can take care of your horse tonight. Why don't you go inside and get some rest."

"I don't know how much resting I'll get accomplished, but I thank you for the offer." He led Beau into a stall and removed his headstall. After giving Beau a pat on the shoulder, he took his leave.

Cookie brushed down his Clydesdale and looked longingly at the door.

"I can take care of your horse, too Sergeant."

"Thanks, Private. I just can't stop thinking about poor Miss Emily, and the corporal. I can't imagine what he must be going through."

"Go keep him company. He probably shouldn't be alone right now."

Cookie nodded and followed the corporal out into the night.

Silent Owl watched as Wilkerson unsaddled Dawson and Beau. "Why do you spend so much time with the horses?"

"I don't reckon I know. Something about them just helps me feel better."

"The Spirits are with you."

"What does that mean again? You keep saying it, but you don't tell me why. How can the Spirits be with me if people keep dying? We've been here almost two weeks and are no closer to stopping the killings."

"You'll have your chance soon enough."

"How do you know that?"

"I listen to the Spirits. They are always talking to us. You just don't know how to hear them." With that, Shaman went to join the others.

David shook his head. *Maybe the corporal is right. This is all just 'mumbo jumbo.'* He finished with the horses and realized something was missing. *Where is the stable boy?*

Wilkerson walked to the feed room, but he wasn't there. He wasn't oiling tack either. David's heart raced in his chest as he frantically threw forage and oats to the horses.

He checked their water and found all the buckets empty. *That isn't like him…*

David fetched a bucket and walked to the back of the livery. He didn't know where the pump was, but he figured it must be back there somewhere. As he groped around, his foot snagged on something, and he landed on his stomach with a thud. The air rushed out of his chest with a *woof.*

The bucket flew out of his hand and landed with a clank. Wilkerson pushed himself to his knees and gasped for breath. As he inhaled, the all too familiar stench of copper assaulted his nostrils.

*No, not again.* He rose slowly to his feet and reached for his revolver. The weight of the weapon in his hand reassured him as he peered into the darkness. David looked down to see what tripped him. His breath caught in his chest, and he suppressed the urge to vomit.

The stable boy was missing no longer. "Why!" David screamed. He dropped to his knees; the bucket forgotten.

"What is all this ruckus about?" Herr Wagner rounded the corner of the building and slid to a stop in a patch of frozen mud. He regained his balance and made his way over to Wilkerson more slowly this time.

David looked up at him and pointed to the water pump. He could not speak; grief and frustration held his tongue.

"Oh, no." Herr Wagner reached down to tousle the stable boy's light brown hair. "He was a good *der Knabe.* What happened?"

"I noticed the horses were out of water, so I came back here to fill the bucket." Wilkerson pointed in the direction the bucket had flown in when he tripped. "I didn't see him lying there, and I tripped over him." David sobbed. "I'm so sorry."

"You didn't do this." Herr Wagner waved his arms in the direction of the stable boy. "That creature is to blame. Come, let's go inside. I'll get Sheriff Nelson and have him tell the undertaker."

Wilkerson nodded numbly and followed the proprietor to the Wagner House. As they meandered around the women praying in the street, a chill settled upon the square. David shivered. The hairs on the back of his neck saluted and his teeth chattered.

"Herr Wagner, I suggest you get these ladies inside."

"Why is that? They are bad for business."

"So is another dead body. Tell the lieutenant I need him, please."

The normally jovial man grimaced and barked at the women to follow him.

"No, thank you! I am not stepping foot inside your unholy establishment." The woman who spoke with Lieutenant Brant earlier stood defiantly with a Bible in the crook of her left arm and her right hand on her hip. She stamped her foot for emphasis.

"Ma'am, I reckon I don't care about your tantrum at the moment. Git inside if you know what's good for you."

"I don't take orders from you, *Private,* and you'll do well to remember that."

A whistle echoed along the street and fog descended around them. "Trust me, Ma'am, you'll be safer inside." In the distance, he heard snarling and the thunder of hoofbeats.

"What is that?" The woman shrieked hysterically and pointed in the distance.

"That is what I'm trying to protect you from! Now get inside!"

A pair of glowing yellow eyes emerged through the fog. The mist parted allowing a creature through and it stalked toward her.

"Oh, Jesus!" She picked up her skirts and ran to the entrance. The other women followed suit and bolted to the door.

"Make way!" Lieutenant Brant barked from inside. "Let us through!"

The terrified women tripped over each other as they shuffled to the door. They bounced off each other's skirts creating a logjam that completely blocked the doorway.

Corporal Miller picked up a barstool and threw it through one of the windows. Shattered glass rained onto the wooden walkway and crunched under boots as the men scrambled through the makeshift opening.

Private Wilkerson stood with his back to the building. He held both revolvers aimed at the creature.

"Form a line," ordered Lieutenant Brant.

The men spread out to make a human wall between the beast and the Wagner House. Each man held a weapon and waited with bated breath for the beast to attack.

The creature paced in front of them, looking for an opening. It lunged toward Cookie, who jerked the trigger of his Dragoon.

The revolver barked, and the boom echoed into the night.

Shaking its head, the beast moved away. It was uninjured.

Silent Owl stood at the end of their line with his tomahawk raised. "Is this the Stonecoat? Or did the Sergeant miss his shot?"

"Do you see any blood?" Corporal Miller turned his head briefly in the Shaman's direction.

"We do not know if this one bleeds." Silent Owl closed his eyes.

Private Wilkerson looked closely at the creature. Once again, he saw a small tuft of red hair atop its head. "Don't shoot!"

"It don't matter if I can't hit the thing!" Cookie's arm shook.

"Red, is that you?" Private Wilkerson lowered his weapon.

"What are you doing, Private?" Lieutenant Brant took a step forward.

"It's alright, Sir. I don't think he'll hurt us."

"Tell that to Emily!" Corporal Miller growled.

"We don't know if Red killed her! Maybe there's another one out here."

"I am not going to bet the lives of the people in this town on your assumption!" Lieutenant Brant took aim.

"Sir, please!"

The beast lunged again.

Wilkerson stepped out of the line. "Red! Stop!"

The creature glanced briefly at Private Wilkerson, and then it jumped at the lieutenant.

Lieutenant Brant fired. The *boom* of his revolver reverberated along the street. Blood blossomed in the middle of the beast's chest. It collapsed in a heap at his feet.

David ran to the creature.

"Private, what are you doing?"

"It's Red, Sir, I just know it!"

Corporal Miller looked at Silent Owl. "What do the spirits say?"

A wagon trundled in their direction. The undertaker stopped his team and waited.

Wilkerson approached the creature and touched its shoulder. Its skin was cold to the touch.

It looked into David's eyes and took a labored breath. It groaned and tried to get up.

David backed away but didn't break eye contact. As he watched, the yellow eyes morphed into green irises. "Red, I knew it was you."

Like Samson, the creature changed shape before his eyes. A couple of heartbeats later, Aiden Flanagan lay naked in the middle of the street with a bullet hole in his chest.

Wilkerson took his hand. "I'm sorry."

Red took a haggard breath. "Sorry for what? This isn't your fault. I'm the one who deserted."

"You didn't desert. You went to find your mare." A tear trickled down David's face.

"I was a fool." Red's eyelids fluttered. "It's okay now. I'll go join her in the afterlife."

"No, don't go. Maybe we can save you."

"There is no saving my body." Red coughed and a dribble of blood ran down his chin. "Is it too late for my soul?"

Wilkerson heard a rustling behind him. The ladies who were praying in the street earlier gathered around them. They raised their arms over David and Red.

In unison, the women recited, "As You send us to them, we pray that You open their eyes, turning them from darkness to light and from the power of Satan unto God, so that they might receive forgiveness of sins and the inheritance, which is sanctified by the faith that is in You Lord Jesus."

David squeezed Red's hand. "Wait for me in Paradise, my friend."

"I will." Red smiled as the light left his eyes.

Wilkerson collapsed to his backside, wrapped his arms around his knees, and bowed his head. Sobs wracked his body.

"Thank you, ladies." Lieutenant Brant walked up behind Wilkerson.

"You can thank us by no longer drinking whiskey. You see what that foul libation does? It turns good men into monsters!"

Another woman added, "We weren't just praying for him." She indicated Red. "We've been praying for all of you."

The undertaker walked over. "Your ministrations are much appreciated this evening. Now, please let us get to work so we can lay this poor soul to rest."

The women huffed but dispersed and walked away into the night.

"Prayer is a powerful thing." Silent Owl looked at Red's body. "The Spirits tell me he will go to a good place."

"He was a good kid." Corporal Miller took a deep breath.

"I don't know about the rest of you, but I'm tired of losing people." Cookie placed a hand on the corporal's shoulder.

Corporal Miller nodded in agreement.

Wilkerson turned his tear-streaked face to the lieutenant. "Sir, this needs to end. How many more people have to die before this will be over?" He sniffed.

"Let's get you inside. Cookie, Corporal, please assist the undertaker with Private Flanagan." Lieutenant Brant offered David his hand.

The private hesitated but took the help and got to his feet. "How much longer until our reinforcements arrive? Waiting around for people to die is madness."

"I agree. We've been defending for too long. It's past time we take the fight to the beasts."

# Chapter Nineteen

Private Wilkerson walked with Lieutenant Brant back inside the Wagner House. Herr Wagner was waiting for them with a glare.

"Who is going to fix my window? The winter chill is chasing my customers away." He huffed.

"In case you didn't notice, we were preoccupied with a monster in the middle of the street." David pointed a finger at the proprietor. "You recall, the one who killed your stable boy!"

Herr Wagner ducked his head. Red blotches spread across his face.

Lieutenant Brant looked at the shattered glass. "When my men return from the undertaker, I'll have them board it up for you," Wagner tensed, "as a temporary measure. Once this wendigo problem is sufficiently solved, we will take responsibility for a more permanent solution." Wagner nodded and walked back behind the bar.

"Herr Wagner!" A dozen women were seated on the far side of the dining room. One of them stood with her Bible in hand. "Don't forget what you promised us."

"Ya, ya," he groused.

"What promise?" Wilkerson asked.

"The ladies say the beast that attacked them was brought here by the Devil himself."

"That's preposterous!" Lieutenant Brant sat on a barstool with a huff.

"Maybe it is, maybe not, all I know is that beast is bad for business."

"What does your promise have to do with the wendigo?" David was afraid of where this was leading.

"The women said if men in town stop imbibing the spirits, the beast will go away. It is our punishment for straying from the word of the Lord."

"And you believe them?" David waved his hand in the direction of the women.

"What I believe does not matter. What matters is keeping my customers happy."

David sighed. "And your promise…"

"I told them I would not serve whiskey again."

Wilkerson hung his head. "My best friend just died in my arms. That beast conscripted him and turned him into a monster. Whiskey has nothing to do with this!"

The leader of the group of ladies walked over to David. "Your friend's soul was saved. Don't despair. He will walk with the Lord in Paradise." With that, she and the rest of the women filed out of the dining room.

*That's great for Red, but I could really use something to calm my nerves.* Wilkerson sighed again.

After the last lady left, Herr Wagner reached under the bar and pulled out a small bottle.

"What is this?" Lieutenant Brant raised an eyebrow.

"Secret stash." Herr Wagner winked. "It's the last of my personal homebrew. I told the ladies I wouldn't 'sell' whiskey anymore. I said nothing about sharing a bottle with associates."

The Lieutenant chuckled as Corporal Miller, Cookie, and Silent Owl walked up to the bar. He poured a small amount of the clear liquid into glasses Herr Wagner placed in front of them.

"Drink up, men! Looks like this is the last drop of liquor we will get to enjoy as long as we remain in Greenville."

"The sooner we leave here, the better." Corporal Miller downed his drink and wiped his mouth with his uniform sleeve.

"Here, here!" Cookie raised his glass and clinked it with Wilkerson's.

David nodded, and said, "For Red."

"For Red," the men echoed.

David sat at the bar with his troop for another hour. They traded stories about Red. Most stories made him laugh, but the last one caused tears to trickle down his face. He sniffed. "Lieutenant, by your leave."

Lieutenant Brant nodded. "Get some rest, Private. We've some planning to do in the morning."

"Yes, Sir." Wilkerson plodded up the stairs, exhaustion pushing on his shoulders and grief weighing down his heart. As he reached the top of the stairs, his breath caught in his chest.

"I found this in your room. Thought you might need it later; it looks important."

Private Wilkerson gulped. The maid from earlier stood outside his door in nothing but a nightdress. Her long brown hair cascaded down her shoulders and ended at her ample hips. Hanging from her finger was a leather cord with his obsidian disc spinning underneath. She curled her finger toward her face.

David's cheeks flushed and his mouth went dry. "Much obliged Ma'am." He coughed. "I thought I'd lost it forever."

"Are you going to make me stand here in the hallway all night, or will you thank me properly?"

"Where are my manners?" Wilkerson unlocked the door, all previous fatigue forgotten.

The maid closed the door and hung his amulet on the knob. She pushed him onto the bed. Pulling at his belt, she said, "Maybe they're hiding in your trousers."

"David… David! Wake up!"

Wilkerson moaned and rolled onto his back. His left arm flopped onto the mattress. "What do you want, Red?" *Red?*

David sat bolt upright in bed. The maid lay sleeping between him and the bedroom window. Silhouetted in the moonlight was his dead friend. His breath caught in his chest and his heart hammered against his ribcage.

Wilkerson reached for his revolver, but it wasn't on the nightstand. He remembered his trousers being pulled down his legs, with his weapons still in his belt. He sighed and rolled to the floor.

"You won't need that. My Master beckons."

"Red, you're dead, remember? And your 'master' doesn't have power over you anymore. The ladies prayed over your soul. The last thing you said to me was that you would wait for me in Paradise."

Red's face changed into an elongated skull with antlers where its ears should be. A gravelly voice boomed, "If you won't come willingly, then I will just have to compel you!" The beast leaped onto the bed and grabbed the still-sleeping maid. Yellow eyes glowed as it turned its gaze to Wilkerson. "I will trade her soul for yours. You know where to find me." It threw the maid over its shoulder.

Wilkerson jumped to his feet and reached for her.

The beast backhanded David and sent him sprawling.

The private scrabbled across the floor and reached for his weapon.

Glass shattered as the beast burst through the window. With speed that defied logic, the creature bounded down the side of the building, bolted across the street, and disappeared into the woods.

Wilkerson's door burst open. "What the Hell happened?" Corporal Miller stood breathless in his long johns. "And why are you nekkid?"

David looked down and blushed. "Get dressed and wake the lieutenant. We can't wait for reinforcements."

# Chapter Twenty

Private Wilkerson grabbed the amulet hanging from his doorknob and placed the leather cord around his neck. He quickly pulled on his trousers and donned his uniform shirt. As he fastened the buttons, the scent of the maid's perfume tickled his nostrils. David inhaled deeply and fought back tears. *We're going to save her. This ends tonight!*

With resolve in his heart, he checked the cylinders of his revolvers and headed down the stairs.

Lieutenant Brant met him on the stairwell. "What happened?"

"The wendigo, Sir. It came to my room just now and took the maid."

"What was she doing in your room?"

David blushed.

"I see." The Lieutenant smirked.

They met the rest of the men in the dining room. "Let's go," said Corporal Miller.

"Hold." The Lieutenant held up his hand. "We need a plan."

"No offense, Sir, but we don't have time! That beast could be eating her right now."

"Eating who?" Cookie looked perplexed as he rubbed the sleep from his eyes.

"Our young Private became a man last night." Miller punched him lightly in the shoulder.

"Did he now?" Cookie beamed.

"Focus, men. We are not going to charge blindly into the woods. The trees are the beast's domain. We must not allow it to set the terms."

"Sir, with respect, where else are we going to fight it? We can't risk any more of the townsfolk."

Lieutenant Brant sighed. "You have a point, Corporal. Any other ideas?"

"What about the reinforcements?" Cookie asked. "Shouldn't they be here by now?"

"It has been a couple of days since I received the telegram and I don't know what has kept them, but Private Wilkerson is right. We can't wait any longer. The maid and the rest of this town are in grave and immediate danger. We must act now!"

Silent Owl grunted. "If what we face is a true Stonecoat, your guns and sabres will not be enough. Perhaps, the only way to stop it is with fire."

"What about your tomahawk? When the beast drooled on Cookie's beard, you said its saliva can make any blade sharper."

Shaman looked at Wilkerson. "Yes, but that is Legend. I know not if it is true in life."

"More mumbo jumbo," Corporal Miller mumbled.

Cookie shuddered and wiped his beard absentmindedly. "I can make us a fire."

"How so?" Lieutenant Brant frowned.

"When I was in the stable earlier, I noticed something covered with a canvas tarp. The stable boy was gone, so I took a peek to see what it was."

"And?"

"Help me hitch it to the wagon and I'll make sure we have a fire." Cookie grinned and winked.

"Very well. Corporal, you will be our guidon bearer. Tonight, we ride into battle!"

Corporal Miller fastened the red over white silk swallow-tailed guidon to its straight-grained ash lance. He secured it with the brass spear point finial. Admiring his handiwork, he rolled the guidon along the polearm and carried it into the stable.

Beau pawed impatiently at the ground with his right front hoof.

"I know, boy. Let's get you saddled."

Miller quickly ran a brush over Beau's withers and back. He placed the saddle on his horse's back and secured the cinch. Checking the stirrup leathers, he tapped Beau on his barrel.

The horse exhaled, so Miller tightened the cinch. "Nice try." The corporal chuckled.

"All right, men. Mount up!" Lieutenant Brant ordered.

Miller quickly slid the bit into Beau's mouth and pulled the headstall over his tippy ears. He led Beau out of the stall and handed the guidon to Cookie.

Cookie held the silk against the pole while Miller mounted his horse. He walked around Beau's hindquarters, placing his right hand on the dock of his tail, so the horse would know he was there. "Ready?"

The corporal took a deep breath and closed his eyes. *For Emily.* He nodded and accepted the guidon from Sergeant Taylor. "We hold the line…"

"…between Heaven and Hell."

After the rest of the men were mounted, Cookie walked over to the wagon. He double-checked the hitch and made sure the Parrott Gun was secured. At a nod from Lieutenant Brant, he climbed onto the buckboard and waited.

A dense fog settled along the street partially obscuring Cookie's view of the mounted men.

"It's here!" Private Wilkerson yelled.

"Where? I don't see anything." Corporal Miller's voice cracked.

In the distance, a shrill whistle echoed in the darkness. Cookie tensed and gooseflesh erupted on his arms. The Clydesdale pulling the wagon reared and galloped down the street.

"Whoa, whoa!" Cookie pulled hard on the reins and the gelding finally stopped. It danced in its harness, the wagon rocking from side to side. "Quit that!"

Lieutenant Brant trotted up to Cookie. "You sure you can handle this?"

"Yes, Sir. Just pre-battle jitters. Looks like he got it out of his system."

"Very well." Lieutenant Brant nodded. "Wait for the rest of us to ride on ahead. You're in trail."

"Yes, Sir."

The lieutenant moved his arm in a circle and the mounted soldiers rode over to him.

"Remember the plan. We need to keep the beast out of the town. Once we get to the woods, be wary. Any sign of movement, sound off. Any questions?"

Another whistle pierced the night.

"Private, that's your cue."

Private Wilkerson gulped.

"Are you sure you're up for this?"

"Sir, that beast has been taunting me since we got here. It's the reason Red died, and it has killed too many people in this town. Now, it has the maid. This ends tonight!"

The lieutenant nodded.

David took a deep breath and said a prayer, "Yea, though I walk through the valley of the shadow of death, I will fear no evil: for thou *art* with me; thy rod and thy staff they comfort me. Thou preparest a table before me in the presence of mine enemies: thou anointest my head with oil; my cup runneth over. Surely goodness and mercy shall follow me all the days of my life: and I will dwell in the house of the LORD for ever."

Silent Owl rode up and reached for David. They grasped forearms and bowed to each other. "Don't forget, the Spirits are with you."

David released Shaman's arm and fondled the obsidian disc amulet around his neck. "I'm ready."

Private Wilkerson squeezed Dawson with his calves and trotted toward the woods. His heart hammered in his chest as he approached the clearing with the rubble of what was once the sugar shack.

"I've been waiting." A disembodied voice floated on the fog. "Patience is not my strong suit."

"That's because patience is a virtue. Something tells me you aren't exactly a virtuous being."

The voice laughed. "Virtue is overrated. I take what I want when I want it. And I want you."

David swallowed. "Why me? You took my friend and now he's dead because of you!" Private Wilkerson spat.

"You have a pure soul. Those are so rare these days."

"Here I am, with my 'pure soul.' You offered a trade. Where is she? Let her go!"

The voice laughed again. "Your female friend was never here. I showed you what you needed to see to lure you to my domain."

If the maid wasn't here, where was she? Was she safe at the Wagner House sleeping peacefully in his bed? If she was truly safe, he didn't have to do this, not tonight anyway.

Wilkerson shook his head. No, she may be safe at the moment, but she wouldn't remain that way. As long as the wendigo threatened the town, no one would be safe. He needed to act, and it needed to be now.

"I'm here now. Show yourself!"

The fog separated and the largest wendigo David had ever seen emerged from the mist. Its yellow eyes glowed ominously at the height of Dawson's withers. It strode forward on four legs and sniffed the air. "Mmm, your fear is delicious." It stood upright, its antlers brushing the canopy of the overhead trees. "I will consume your flesh and then your soul will become mine."

"I don't think so!" Lieutenant Brant took a knee to Wilkerson's left and fired at the creature with his Sharps rifle. "Advance!"

Corporal Miller lowered the guidon and kicked Beau in the flank. The gelding charged forward; ears pinned against his head.

Silent Owl raised his tomahawk and drove his war pony forward.

Private Wilkerson unholstered two of his revolvers and pointed Dawson at the threat. His horse ran up the middle as Corporal Miller and Silent Owl's mounts closed the distance. Lining up his sights, David thumbed the hammer of his left revolver first, then the right. Using his legs to keep Dawson steady, he squeezed the trigger; left, right, *boom, boom!* Smoke filled the air adding to the haze created by the fog. The bullets bounced off the creature's thick hide as Dawson cantered past it.

As the mounted men regrouped, the beast snarled. "A fight, is it? Then a fight you will have!" It jumped forward and raced toward Lieutenant Brant's position.

The lieutenant fired again, aiming square in the middle of the beast's chest. *Boom!* The sound reverberated throughout the clearing and echoed across the night.

Once again, the wendigo suffered no injury. "That tickled," it taunted as it reached within a few feet of the lieutenant.

Private Wilkerson kicked Dawson's sides and they sprinted at the beast. The ground raced by as they thundered across the clearing. Just as the creature was about to plow through Lieutenant Brant, Dawson body-checked him. Beast and horse flew through the air and landed in a heap. Private Wilkerson was thrown clear of the saddle and ended up next to the lieutenant. He struggled for breath and fought to get back on his feet.

Dawson rolled to his hooves and snorted as he trotted to his rider.

Shaking his head and wiping the mud from his trousers, David hauled himself back into the saddle. "Sir, are you well?"

Lieutenant Brant stood staring wide-eyed at the wendigo. His mouth worked, but no sound came out.

"Sir! Snap out of it."

The Lieutenant shook his head. "I didn't realize they could move so fast…"

Silent Owl and Corporal Miller rode over. "I told you the guns would have no effect." Shaman looked at the lieutenant. "It is a true Stonecoat."

"So, we need fire?" Private Wilkerson looked to where the beast lay.

"Yes."

Lieutenant Brant rolled his shoulders and stretched his neck from side to side. "Then fire we shall have."

Cookie waited at the edge of the tree line. Gunshots and thundering hooves sounded from the clearing, and he wanted nothing more than to help his brothers in arms. He knew he would get his chance soon enough.

He walked to the rear of the wagon and unhitched the ten-pound Parrott Gun. Then he unhitched his Clydesdale from the wagon. Cookie grabbed the horse's reins and walked him to the artillery piece. He hitched the horse to the gun and led him through the trees along a path wide enough for the wheels of the cart.

"Dammit, we're pointing the wrong way!" Cookie turned the horse and gun around, with difficulty, as his horse kept nibbling at the grass poking its way through the frozen ground. "You can graze later!"

Once the Parrott Gun was in position, the sergeant tied his Clydesdale to a stout tree and headed back to the wagon. Herr Wagner was waiting for him.

Cookie stopped short. "What are you doing here?"

"I thought you could use a hand."

"What do you know about artillery?"

Herr Wagner laughed. "Enough to know you cannot load and fire this gun by yourself. Besides, you found this in my stable, no?"

Cookie smiled. "Grab a shell and follow me."

Wagner grabbed a 9.5-pound shell and the sponge-rammer.

Cookie picked up the powder and a bucket.

"Don't forget the fuse wire." Wagner winked at Cookie.

"Maybe you know more about this than I do."

Herr Wagner chuckled. He reached into his pocket and pulled out a breech sight.

Cookie rolled his eyes and walked back to the gun. He put the sponge into the bucket and swabbed out the barrel.

Wagner placed his thumb over the vent. He winked at Cookie.

"You really do know more than you're letting on."

"Let's just say I'm glad we are working together to get rid of the monster attacking my town." He pointed to the shell.

Cookie picked up the shell and inspected the percussion fuse. Seeing no signs of wear or defect, he slid the shell into the gun. He used the wooden rammer to shove the shell as far into the gun as possible.

Wagner punctured the cartridge and waited for Cookie to sight the Parrott Gun.

Cookie lined up the sight, then attached the lanyard to a friction primer. He inserted the primer into the vent.

Once again, Wagner covered the vent with his thumb.

Cookie pulled the lanyard taut and waited.

Herr Wagner stepped clear.

Once the lieutenant gave the command, they would be able to fire.

The beast stirred and jumped to its feet. It snarled and roared at the men. "Is that the best you can do? Knock me down with your pathetic horse?"

Lieutenant Brant jumped into the saddle. "Alright, men, here is what we're going to do. Mounted charge, on the guidon. Corporal Miller, that's you."

The corporal nodded and moved to the left. Lieutenant Brant lined up on him, followed by Private Wilkerson, and Silent Owl at the far right.

The lieutenant took a deep breath. "Men, forward. Guide, left. March!"

Four horses walked in a line toward the beast.

"Is this supposed to frighten me?" The creature stood its ground.

"Trot – march!"

The mounts picked up speed, sending the fog swirling around their pumping legs.

"Gallop – march!"

Hoofbeats thundered throughout the clearing, rivaling the sound of drums the men heard when they first encountered the creature weeks ago.

"Charge!"

Private Wilkerson and the lieutenant leveled their revolvers. They pulled their triggers simultaneously. *Boom!*

The creature staggered but remained upright. "I've had enough of this!" The wendigo leaped over the charging column and landed behind them, claws raking through the frozen ground. "Do you want to play, or do you want to fight?"

Lieutenant Brant spun his horse around. He leveled his revolver and fired again. Sparks blossomed upon the creature's chest as the round ricocheted off its impenetrable hide. "Now would be a good time for a *fire!*" He yelled the last, so loud he felt as if his throat was being ripped out from the inside.

The wendigo bounded toward him in a flash.

The lieutenant turned his horse away from the monster, but it was too late. He felt a warm trickle work its way down his chest. As he looked down, fierce claws poked through his neck. Blood poured onto his hands and down his trousers. *So, this is the end.*

The talons ripped their way out the same way they had come. Lieutenant Brant's vision swam, and he slumped in the saddle, sliding onto the ground.

"Now would be a good time for a *fire!*"

"That's the signal!" Cookie yanked the lanyard. The Parrott Gun rocked with the force of the explosion and rolled backward about three feet.

Cookie's Clydesdale screamed and pulled free of the tree he was tied to. He galloped off in the direction of the town.

"Let's hope the first shell hits its target. It will be hard to move the gun without a horse."

Cookie watched as the projectile slammed into the detritus of the old sugar shack. The ground shook and his ears rang. He felt the concussive force of the blast hit his chest, as tree branches swayed dangerously around him. Small rocks and clumps of mud rained down on him and Herr Wagner. Splinters flew all around them and embedded themselves in the gun's wooden cart.

"Get down!" Herr Wagner pulled him to the ground, just as a massive tree fell across the trail. It landed on the Parrott Gun, sending the wheels of the cart rolling away.

"You saved me. Thank you!"

"You may have helped save this town. It's the least I could do."

They both stood and watched as flames rose into the sky, sending sparks dancing across the night.

"You wanted a fire, Sir. You have a fire."

Corporal Miller didn't have time to process the loss of his superior officer. No sooner did the lieutenant's body hit the ground, the earth shook, and Beau reared up in panic. In his shock, the corporal lost his seat, and the guidon flew out of his grasp.

He ran after Beau, but the horse was too fast. Corporal Miller turned around and saw the raging conflagration that was the sugar shack. Silent Owl said that fire was the only possible way to stop a Stonecoat, but how would they get the beast to willingly walk through the flames?

Smoke billowed into the night sky. Miller coughed and covered his mouth and nose with the crook of his arm. As he got closer, the firelight reflected off something metal in the distance. That gave the corporal an idea.

*I will avenge you tonight my darling.*

Private Wilkerson patted Dawson on the withers, but to no avail. His terrified gelding saw Beau heading back to the stable, and he wanted to go, too. David leaned forward as Dawson reared, but as soon as his front hooves touched the ground, he lifted them back into the air.

Wilkerson waited for Dawson to touch down again, then performed an emergency dismount. He swung his right leg over the back of his cantle as he pulled his left foot out of the stirrup. He hung his belly momentarily over Dawson's back, then slid swiftly to his feet. As soon as his boots touched the earth, Dawson bolted out of the clearing to follow his herd mate.

David watched his horse flee to safety, then heard hoofbeats behind him. Silent Owl's war pony didn't seem afraid and neither did the Shaman.

Silent Owl watched the other horses flee to the perceived safety of the stable. His pony knew better. She understood this beast had to be stopped here and now, or it would wreak havoc on this plane for eternity.

The Shaman bowed his head and spoke briefly with the Spirits. When he opened his eyes, he knew what he needed to do.

Silent Owl squeezed his pony with his legs and urged her forward. She sprang toward the beast and raced in its direction.

The beast met her with a slash of its claws and raked her along the neck. Blood fountained from the gashes and splashed her legs.

She stumbled and rolled sending Silent Owl to the ground.

Shaman rose slowly and stalked toward the beast with his tomahawk raised. From his right, Private Wilkerson came running into the fray.

"Ah, there he is. Are you ready to join me, or do I have to kill all your friends and save you for last?"

Private Wilkerson pointed his revolvers at the beast. "I will never join you."

"Then their fate is sealed!" The Stonecoat slashed at Silent Owl.

Shaman managed to dodge the strike but overbalanced and fell onto his back. He lost his grip on the tomahawk, and it flew into the air, landing a few feet away from him.

The beast lunged at Silent Owl.

Wilkerson's heart hammered in his chest. He unloaded his revolvers again and again, but they had no effect on the creature. His revolvers empty, he dropped them on the ground and unsheathed his sabre. *If this is how I die, at least I will go out fighting.*

"Tsk, tsk. Your guns didn't work. You really think your little sword can hurt me?"

Corporal Miller moved stealthily to the guidon. Its silk field melted in the fire, and the brass finial glowed with intense heat. Carefully, he lifted the wooden pole from the fire, flames bursting from the opposite side.

He coughed, the stench of the melting silk mixing with the remains of the sugar shack was almost too much to bear. Corporal Miller cleared his throat. He looked over to where Wilkerson and the creature stood.

"You really think your little sword can hurt me?" The creature taunted the private.

"Maybe not, but this will!" Miller tucked the guidon pole against his left side and ran for all he was worth. Sparks erupted in front of him as he closed the distance to the beast.

The creature's eyes grew wide, and he made to fling the corporal away.

Private Wilkerson got there first. The beast's arm connected with Wilkerson's chest and sent him spinning. He landed breathlessly next to Silent Owl.

Corporal Miller screamed, "This is for Emily!" He used all of his momentum and plunged the burning brass spear point into the wendigo's chest. The molten metal spear pierced the creature's heart, flash-boiling the ice inside. A hiss of steam escaped as the creature fell to its knees.

It roared in agony and desperation.

Wilkerson crawled to Silent Owl's tomahawk. If the Legend was right, this was his only time to act. As long as the beast was weakened by fire, he stood a chance. David grasped the weapon by its handle and jogged behind the wendigo. Using all the strength he had left, he raised the tomahawk and brought it down on the creature's neck, just like chopping wood when he was a young boy.

The wendigo's head fell from its neck and rolled to Corporal Miller's feet. The tomahawk lodged itself in the frozen ground.

Private Wilkerson collapsed. It was over.

The wendigo shrank and morphed into a human.

David looked at the head and the face resolved into none other than the undertaker. He started to gag and vomited onto the ground.

Corporal Miller picked up the head by its hair. "Who would of thought; it was the undertaker this whole time?"

Wilkerson shook his head and heaved again.

A dark cloud emerged from the undertaker's sawn neck. It floated above the flames and resolved into the shape of a man with antlers where his ears should be.

"You may have stopped me this time, but you didn't kill me, not my spirit form, anyway. We will meet again Private David Wilkerson. And when we do, your soul *will* be mine."

"My soul is already spoken for!"

"Insolent little humans! You know nothing of the power I command. I was a member of the Council on Etashn'ish. I have lived longer than you can possibly fathom! You can't ever stop me.." The spirit of the wendigo drifted away like so much smoke.

# Chapter Twenty-One

"That was strange." Corporal Miller dusted himself off as the first rays of dawn broke through the darkness of the clearing.

"You're telling me." Private Wilkerson stood and wiped his mouth with the back of his hand. "Are you alright?"

"Yeah, I think so." Corporal Miller dropped the undertaker's head next to his decapitated body. "At least I'm doing better than him."

Wilkerson rolled his eyes and looked over to Silent Owl. He was on his knees next to his war pony, his hands on her neck muttering something to himself.

David staggered over next to him. Not knowing what to do, he knelt to place his hand on the horse's wither and closed his eyes.

Shaman continued muttering in his native Algonquin tongue. A soft nicker emanated from the small mare, and she lifted her head off the ground.

"The Spirits say she will recover." Silent Owl stood and offered David his hand.

Private Wilkerson accepted the assistance and asked, "What did you do?"

"I asked the Spirits to heal her. She fought with us to vanquish the Stonecoat. The Spirits agreed she was worthy."

Corporal Miller tsked. "More mumbo jumbo."

"Don't be such a skeptic. Like Shaman said, there is much about our world we do not understand."

Silent Owl grunted in assent.

"Where's Lieutenant Brant?" Cookie burst through the tree line and ran up to the assembled men.

Corporal Miller pointed to their fallen officer. "He was a good man."

A tear slid down Cookie's face. He made his way to the lieutenant and placed his hand over the man's eyes. "Silent Owl, is there anything you can do?"

"Sadly, no. He fought well and Our Grandmother will gather him into her net and escort him to Heaven."

"We need to call the undertaker."

"He's over there." Wilkerson pointed to the body lying next to the smoking bonfire.

"Well, I'll be d—"

"I didn't see that one coming, either." Corporal Miller clapped Cookie on his back.

The men stood there somberly, not knowing what to say.

A whistling broke the silence. Each man reached for a weapon and leveled it at the approaching threat.

"Whoa, I'm here to help!" Sheriff Nelson walked out of the woods with his hands up. "I ran into Herr Wagner on the road, and he told me where to find you. What happened?"

Private Wilkerson filled him in on the events of the previous night and early morning. The sheriff whistled again. "I'll go inform his family," he indicated the undertaker's body, "and get one of his apprentices to retrieve him."

"Thank you, Sheriff." Wilkerson offered his hand.

"We also need to take care of Lieutenant Brant." Corporal Miller ran his hand through his ash-covered hair. "Cookie, where is your wagon?"

"It's down that trail." He pointed in the direction he had come from. "But my horse ran off when the artillery shell detonated."

"The horses!" Wilkerson remembered how Dawson and Beau ran off before their battle with the Stonecoat.

"It's alright. Joseph can pull a wagon." The Sheriff walked down the trail and indicated for the cavalrymen to follow him.

Cookie hitched Joseph to the wagon and climbed onto the buckboard. He made to flick the reins over his back when Sheriff Nelson said, "I'll drive."

Sheepishly, Cookie handed over the reins. "Habit. Sorry."

"No offense taken." The Sheriff chuckled and clucked his tongue.

The wagon moved down the trail and onto the road back into Greenville proper.

Silent Owl led his war pony behind the wagon with Wilkerson walking alongside.

"Are you sure she'll recover?" Wilkerson patted the mare gently on her cheek.

"The Spirits have spoken. Who am I to question their wisdom?"

David caressed the obsidian disc hanging around his neck.

As the men entered town, there was a throng of people waiting to receive them. Whoops and cheers emanated from the crowd along with clapping and shouts of "Here, here!"

The sheriff pulled back on the reins and the wagon came to a halt in front of the livery. Herr Wagner greeted the men. "Your horses are safe in the barn. I gave them oats and forage and made sure their water buckets were full."

"Thank you, Sir." David offered his hand. "There is one more thing you can do for us."

"*Was ist das?*" Herr Wagner raised an eyebrow.

"We need to send a message. Is there a courier handy?"

"No courier is needed, Private."

Wilkerson turned to face the new voice. A tall man with salt and pepper hair and a neatly trimmed beard approached. David sketched a crisp salute. "Captain McLellan."

"As you were," the captain stopped a few paces away. "We arrived just this morning and it looks like we missed all the fun."

"I don't know that I'd call it 'fun', Sir."

"Perhaps not, but your mission was successful. Herr Wagner here says the beast is gone."

"Yes, Sir. We were able to defeat it in the woods…for now."

"Mmm, I don't like the sound of that."

"Nor do I, Sir. Nor do I."

"Tend to your horses then come inside for breakfast. We'll debrief shortly."

"Yes, Sir."

Wilkerson and Corporal Miller walked into the livery to make certain Dawson and Beau were hale. Cookie followed them to check on his Clydesdale.

Sheriff Nelson unhitched Joseph from Cookie's wagon and made to mount up.

"Hold, please." Captain McLelland walked over.

"How may I be of assistance?" The sheriff turned to face him.

"I understand I have a lieutenant in need of last rites."

"His body is in the back of the wagon. I will send someone over to collect him."

"Please send over the pastor instead. We will have him sent back to his family in Missouri."

"Understood, Sir." The sheriff nodded and hoisted himself into the saddle.

"One more thing, Sheriff."

"Yes?"

"I don't want any of my men to be dispatched here again. Is that clear?"

The sheriff nodded and turned Joseph in the direction of the Church. As he rode away, he whistled a catchy tune.

Private Wilkerson brushed his horse down and cleaned his hooves. Using his knife, he picked out a few small pebbles from Dawson's frog. When he was done, Dawson nipped playfully at his hand. "I'm happy to see you, too." David reached into his pocket and pulled out a sugar cube. Dawson licked it off his hand and nickered in appreciation.

With one more pat on the withers for good measure, Wilkerson headed inside the Wagner House. The scent of fried bacon and maple syrup greeted him. Stomach growling, he pulled out a seat and plopped down.

A beautiful young lady with long brown hair brought him a plate overflowing with pancakes and scrambled eggs. "It's good to see you again."

David jumped out of his chair and threw his arms around her. Her perfume tickled his nose and caused his eyes to water with relief. He sniffed. "And you."

She returned his embrace and whispered, "Not here. Meet me in the stable after you eat."

Wilkerson nodded and returned to his chair. He picked up a fork and dove into his breakfast, devouring the buttery pancakes with relish.

Herr Wagner came over. "Is good, ya?"

"So good," David said with a full mouth. "Thank you."

Cookie sat next to him and helped himself to a pile of bacon. "I'm happy to be done with this town, but I am going to miss the food."

"Same here." Corporal Miller reached for the coffee and filled a mug.

Herr Wagner brought over more eggs and another pot of coffee. "Eat up, you all deserve it."

"I concur." The captain came over to their table. The men made to stand, but the captain waved them off. "Please, eat. You've all had a rough night."

He pulled out an empty chair and sat. Looking around the room, he spoke softly. "Tell me what happened here."

The men looked at each other, not knowing where to begin.

"Sergeant, that's an order."

As the highest-ranking member of their troop, Cookie spoke. "We came here to keep order in the town at the request of Governor Noyes. He was worried about the ladies and their temperance crusade causing problems here as they did in New Vienna."

"I heard about that. What I want to know is what else you encountered here."

Corporal Miller cleared his throat. "It turns out the 'crusade' was the least of our problems. A beast had been attacking livestock in the town as well as people. It went after people we had come to care about during our stay here." He dropped his gaze and took a deep breath.

Private Wilkerson continued. "Lieutenant Brant told us about a 'Special Unit' tasked with defeating unearthly creatures, so we followed his lead and went after a Stonecoat."

"He did, did he? He wasn't supposed to divulge that." Captain McLelland pursed his lips.

"Maybe not, Sir, but it's a good thing he did. If it wasn't for Silent Owl and his insight, we might still not know what the beast truly was."

Shaman picked that moment to join them. He offered his hand to the captain.

"Silent Owl, it's good to see you again."

"Wait, you two know each other?" Private Wilkerson sat up straight with his eyes wide.

Shaman chuckled. "Who do you think recruited me to help you in the first place?"

The captain sighed. "We have been receiving reports of these cannibalistic beings throughout the territories.

Something about the fallout of the war attracted them here. As many as we banish back to where they originated, more keep emerging. That's why I'm here."

Cookie spluttered, "We thought you were our reinforcements."

The captain shook his head. "Your reinforcements haven't reported for over a week. We fear they were lost on their last campaign."

Wilkerson slumped his shoulders. "What does this mean for us, Sir?"

"Now that you've seen and fought one of these creatures, we need you to join us. Our Special Unit is dedicated to holding the line—"

"Between Heaven and Hell." The men echoed.

The captain chuckled. "I see Lieutenant Brant shared that with you, too."

"Yes, Sir. He did." Wilkerson sighed.

"Speaking of the lieutenant, we need to bury him." Cookie reached for another cup of coffee.

"I will take care of that. We will send him back to his family. He would want to be reunited with them." The captain raised his mug for Cookie to fill it.

"Reunited, Sir?" Wilkerson asked.

"He didn't tell you how he came to join the Special Unit?"

"No, Sir. It never came up in conversation."

"I'm afraid that isn't my story to tell." The captain took a sip of coffee. "Finish your meals and say your goodbyes. Tomorrow, we continue west." With that, the captain stood and walked outside.

"What if we don't want to join you?" Corporal Miller called after Captain McLelland.

"That is why they are called orders, Son."

Private Wilkerson wiped his mouth with a napkin and headed to the livery. He brought Dawson an apple which the horse inhaled with delight.

"It took you long enough. I was beginning to think you forgot about me." The maid stood in the hay loft wearing nothing but a smile.

David climbed the ladder to join her. "I didn't mean to keep you waiting. The captain has new orders for us."

"What does that mean?"

"It means I have to leave tomorrow."

She pouted and turned away from him. Turning her face back to him, she said, "I guess we'll need to make the most of what little time we have together."

Wilkerson walked over to her and wrapped her in his arms. "I'll miss you."

"Miss me later. Right now, I need you to love me."

Private Wilkerson kissed the maid fiercely and got out of bed. Last night had been the best of his life. This morning wasn't too bad, either. "Come with me."

"I can't. I have a life here." The maid sighed.

"I just realized I don't even know your name." He grinned sheepishly.

"Abigail."

"A name as beautiful as you are." He dressed quickly and leaned down to give her one more peck on the cheek.

"You say that now, but you'll forget all about me as soon as you get back on your horse."

"I could never forget about you. As soon as this mission is over, I'll come back for you."

"You better not keep me waiting."

After a hasty breakfast, the men assembled outside the livery. Their new captain rode in the wagon with Cookie. "We'll make a quick stop for supplies, then head west."

They arrived in front of the G.A. Katzenberger & Bro. store where the proprietor waited on the front porch.

"Captain, I'm sorry to hear about your lieutenant. He seemed a good man."

"That he was. He will be missed." The captain removed his hat and ducked his head. After a moment of silence, he continued. "The best way to celebrate his memory is to finish what he started." He placed his hat back atop his head. "I trust you have the supplies we requested."

"Yes, Sir. Everything is here. I even packed a few extra items. I hope you don't mind."

"I brought these special just for you." Annie emerged from the store with a sack. "You still like rabbits?"

"Boy, do we!" Cookie rubbed his hands together with glee.

"Thank you, Miss Annie." Corporal Miller tipped his hat.

She blushed and curtsied. "After what you all did for the town, it's the least I could do."

Mr. Katzenberger placed a hand on her shoulder. "All right young lady, these boys need to get on their way."

"Yessir." She waved at the men as she walked back toward her home.

"That 'lil lady sure is something." Corporal Miller waved back at her.

"Any lady who can hunt rabbits is just dandy in my book." Cookie beamed.

After the wagon was loaded, the captain turned to Wilkerson. "I'd like you to be our guidon bearer."

"I'd be honored, Sir." David accepted the guidon and moved to the front of the formation.

"March!"

The men headed west away from the rising sun and into their next adventure.

# Epilogue

Sheriff Nelson dismounted and tied Joseph to the hitching post outside his office. He whistled as he unlocked the door and walked inside. As he approached his desk, he noticed the lower drawer was open. Papers lined the floor and Sheriff Moses Scott's journal was nowhere to be found.

He pushed his chair next to the desk and crossed the room. Catching his reflection in the window, he paused. Glowing yellow eyes greeted him.

The sheriff's breath caught in his throat. "You again?"

A black cloud emerged and coalesced into a large bipedal shape with an elongated face. Antlers sprouted where ears should be. "Were you expecting someone else?"

"No. You told me years ago you would come for me. I didn't think it would be this soon." The sheriff walked back to his chair and sat. He stretched his arm toward the scattergun he kept under his desk.

"You failed me. I brought you under my tutelage to build up an army of wendigo. Now, the few you managed to convert are all dead." The creature moved closer to the sheriff. "All except for you."

"I brought you the undertaker. He kept you fed all these years."

"Bah! I'm the one who kept you fed. When you were starving in that shack you called a home, who showed you the way to never starve again?"

"You made me eat my wife. My son!" Rage erupted in the sheriff's chest. His heart rate increased and the pounding in his skull threatened to split his cranium.

"I didn't make you do anything you weren't already predisposed to do." The creature moved to a chair and sat with his lower legs crossed. "I merely made it easier for you to see what had to be done. I showed you how to survive!"

"You call this survival?" The sheriff stood and opened his arms wide to his sides. "No matter how much I eat, I'm never satisfied. My stomach growls constantly. I drink, and no amount of whiskey calms the beast that lives inside my soul."

"At least you are alive."

"Hah! You call this a life? Being a slave to your bidding. Finding other lost souls and delivering them to their fate. This isn't life; this is a death sentence." The sheriff moved back to his desk. He pulled out the scattergun and aimed it at the creature.

The creature laughed. "You think your long gun can hurt me? Have you learned nothing?"

Sheriff Nelson dropped his right arm and placed the barrel of his shotgun under his throat. "I know how to hurt you. I'm your slave no more!" He stared the creature in the eyes and pulled the trigger.

"Pity." The creature stood and walked over to the sheriff's still-warm corpse. "Even though you can no longer serve me in life, you will be useful in death." He bent down and started to eat. Once he had his fill, he wiped his mouth on the sheriff's coat and stalked to the door.

"Sheriff? Sheriff Nelson, are you here?"

The creature called out mimicking the dead sheriff's voice. "I'm not decent. What do you need?"

"Men!" The woman sighed and tried the door. It was locked. "I came to make a request."

"Go ahead, I can hear you just fine."

"The ladies and I have reached an agreement with the hotel keepers and saloon owners. They will no longer sell whiskey because of that creature that threatened the people of this town. They understand their evil ways have caused the Lord to forsake us and that is why the beast preyed upon us."

"The beast was killed. It can't hurt anyone else."

"Maybe so, but what about another beast? If we don't forsake all forms of evil, what's to say the Lord won't send another beast to test our faith? They understand how important this is and they swore to not enter into further temptation."

"Have they now?"

"Yessir. I just wanted to let you know, in case anyone else gets any bright ideas about making their own homebrews. Their actions will cause the wrath of the Lord to descend upon them, and the rest of us innocents as well."

"I see. Have you told the mayor of this new development?"

"I wanted to call on you first before I take this to the mayor."

"Very well. I will uphold my oath to protect the people of Greenville."

"Thank you, Sheriff."

The woman turned on her heel and marched in the direction of City Hall.

*This will complicate things,* the wendigo thought. *With the sheriff out of the picture, people will ask more questions than I want to answer. My minions are dead. Perhaps it is time for me to move on to greener pastures.*

The wendigo shrank back into the mist, a whistling note dancing on the dust motes that hung in the air.

The End

We hope that you enjoyed this title and look forward to many more to come. Please, leave us a review! Reviews matter to all of our authors.

Take a look at some of our other award-winning series at https://threeravenspublishing.com/series-universes/

Visit us at https://www.threeravenspublishing.com and sign up for our newsletter for the latest and greatest news on upcoming titles and events.

Other series and titles you might enjoy.

DECLAN FINN
DECLAN FINN
DECLAN FINN
DECLAN FINN
Demons are Forever
LOVE AT FIRST BITE
Honor at Stake
LOVE AT FIRST BITE ONE
Live and Let Bite
LOVE AT FIRST BITE THREE
Good to the Last Drop
LOVE AT FIRST BITE FOUR
The Dragon Award Nominated Series
FREE on Kindle Unlimited!

AVAILABLE ON
AMAZON
JOINT TASK FORCE
13
AFTER CARLISLE & IMPEACHER
HOLDING THE LINE
BETWEEN HEAVEN AND HELL
13

MYSTERY,
MAGIC &
MAYHEM
WITH A TWIST
OF ROMANCE
J.F. POSTHUMUS
ON AMAZON
FIND ME
B.E.N.T.
BIOLOGIC    ENHANCED    NASCENT    TALENT

THE RAVEN AND THE CROW
MICHAEL K. FALCIANI
FIND ME
ON AMAZON

STARFLIGHT

IT CAME FROM THE
TRAILER PARK

3R
Three Ravens Publishing
Are you looking for fun, new fiction?
The Written Word Will Never Be The Same…
https://www.threeravenspublishing.com
Veteran Owned and Operated

And don't forget to check out the latest edition of *Car Wars*

http://www.sjgames.com/car-wars/

Or the other amazing titles from
Steve Jackson Games

http://www.sjgames.com

…or the latest in the Car Warriors: Autoduel Chronicle fiction series.
https://threeravenspublishing.com/car-warriors-autoduel-chronicles/

You can also keep up to date with our latest release announcements on Scifi.radio and get some of the best fandom programing on the planet.

**Scifi for your Wifi**

And don't forget to check out our other Sponsors and Affiliates

A southern Appalachian jewel for craft beer lovers, Buck Bald Brewing offers something for everyone. With delicious, locally brewed beverages from across the spectrum, Buck Bald Brewing offers craft brews that are consistently amazing.

From the dark and smooth Shesquatch Scottish ale, to the intense hops of Hippibilly IPA, to the puckering sour of the blackberry and cinnamon in Berry My Heart at the Trailer Park, and more than 60+ rotating brews, you'll find what you're looking for and more.

With smiling faces behind the bar ready to help you find your next favorite brew, a constantly rotating selection of delicious craft beverages, toe-tapping tunes always playing, and the biggest games on TV, you can kick your feet up in either Copperhill, Tennessee or Murphy, North Carolina and immerse yourself in the Buck Bald Brewing experience. So, come out, fill a pint, fill a growler, and fill your mind at your new favorite family-owned craft brewery.

To discover more visit us at buckbaldbrewing.com or follow us on Facebook @buckbaldbrewing and @buckbaldbrewingmurphy.

Vesper Wren's
TRAILER PARK
PIXIE
PUNCH
· A PEACH STRAWBERRY SELTZER ·
BUCK BALD BREWING